Mad Moon

Alissa C. Miles

For my family

1

Jo
1986

Mama says I'm the fighting kind. Even in her belly, always trying to find a way out in to the world so that I could start being somebody. I came early and there was nobody to get her to the hospital. Daddy was *gone,* out doing something, I guess. She always left that part out of the story. I don't know much about how babies come out. I've heard some things, girls talking at school, so I have an idea, but it doesn't seem to make much sense, like how do you carry a baby in your stomach? On TV, most women are in hospital beds. They have sweaty foreheads. They scream and the doctors and nurses try to calm them down and then a shiny new pink baby is wrapped up in blankets and handed over to the mother. I think how big and smooth that baby looks for being new. I remember when David came home and he was all little and wrinkly and looked like an old person. I asked Mama if she was sure this baby was the right one and did she mean to bring this one home. And on TV the daddies are there holding the mothers' hands and kissing the mothers' faces and saying how proud they are of her. Proud of what, anyway?

One thing I'm sure of is there's pain. That's how come I wonder how Mama did it on her own, give birth to me on the kitchen floor, right on the tiles. She was trying to get ahold of Aunt Di on the phone in the kitchen when she felt me coming. She says she just hunkered down in the pantry in between the rows of canned tomatoes and black eyed peas and prayed for me to come on if that's the way it was going to go. Once, while Mama was busy with laundry and David was sleeping on the couch, I went into the kitchen and sat on the floor. I sat there cross-legged and then slid down until I was laying with my cheek pressed against the cool tiles. I looked around at the cobwebs underneath the cabinets, the crumbs, the dirty floor. Why did I choose here? What was so special about here that I just had to come right at that moment? I wish I could remember.

I stared at those same tiles on the kitchen floor while police officers talked with Mama and Aunt Di at the kitchen table. I could see them from the couch in the living room, which is where Mama told me to sit. Jo, you sit in here just for a bit. I'll be fine. I wanted to be with her. I couldn't hear what they were saying, but Mama looked worried and sad. She would sit down for a minute and then get up and pace around some more.

Di looked happy. What does she have to be happy about? No one else is happy. Maybe she was thinking of something funny. I do that sometimes. I will be in class at school and my teacher will be talking but I don't hear what she is saying. I am dreaming about having my own horse and riding him around in a big field and petting his coat and giving him carrots to eat. That makes me happy. I doubt Di is thinking about my horse. All she seems to think about are everybody else's problems and how she thinks she knows better.

2

Whatever it is the officers are telling Mama, it seems like something Di wanted to hear. I saw her smile at the police lady like she'd told a good joke. It must be about Daddy and that makes me mad. She shouldn't be happy about Mama and Daddy fighting. 'Cause it can't lead to anything good.

Mama looked over at me and told me to take my brother outside to play. David didn't talk much, which was good because then you can think. It's hard to think when someone is always talking.

David, you shouldn't poke at those worms, I said. You're almost two years old now, for goodness sake. Here draw with this stick and let me sit here on this step and think. I got some thinking to do, okay?

I wanted to come up with some way to fix what Daddy'd done. But, what happened? The police were looking for him. He hadn't come home in two days. I wondered what he'd been eating this whole time and where he was sleeping. I told myself that I didn't really care. Maybe he tried to rob a liquor store or a bank. Maybe he was angry at me for being an extra mouth to feed. I always tried not to eat very much, though, and never asked for anything special when Mama went to the store for groceries. She bought cookies for us once and Daddy threw them against the wall yelled, You think I'm made of money? I almost asked if he was so worried about money, why buy the beer? But I knew better. It is hard to sleep after having your face slapped. Maybe Daddy had done something awful like hurt somebody or killed someone. Could he do that? I thought it over. I pictured him, his dark hair thick and shiny, combed over to the side and his brown eyes; his nose straight and pointed and his jaw working back and forth showing off the squareness of it. He'd be in jeans and an undershirt, his plaid shirt over it and open with the arms rolled up to the elbow, steel-toed work boots. A belt. And, yes, he could if he was madder than ever he probably could kill. I imagined him standing over someone's body with a gun, with a broken beer bottle, with his fists, and saw his face sweaty and red, his hair falling in front and saw his eyes about to pop out of his skull. I shivered. Yelled at David, Quit squishing the worms!

I looked at Mama through the screen door. Her eyes were still. I couldn't tell if she was breathing. The officers talked on and on. I had this feeling. I wanted to march into the kitchen and take Mama by the hand and make her go lie down. Whenever I am upset, she makes me lie down and sometimes she will lie down with me. It makes things better just to lie in the bed a minute. You gotta get all the way in the bed and pull the covers up to your chin and take a few deep breaths. Even if you're not tired you got to get all the way in. That's what I thought Mama needed right then. And I wanted to shout at Di to get out of here and leave us alone. I needed to talk to those policemen and I wanted them to be honest. I'm a kid, but I can take it.

I saw Di hold a hand up to the police to stop them from talking. She walked out the screen door and took me by the shoulders out into the yard. I shrugged her off and she bent down so that her eyes were looking directly in mine. She said, Hey. It's okay. She's okay. She gave me a few dollars and told me to run up the road to the gas station to pick her up a pack of Camels and a couple of candy bars. You know the ones. I nodded. Yeah, I knew the ones Go on then, she said, but I did not go right away. I stood there wanting to refuse to leave Mama, but Di told me to do what she said and I figured it would upset Mama more if I didn't do what Di wanted. I ran to the station. It isn't far from the house. There's a clam shell in the parking lot. A big pink one made out of concrete. It even has a concrete pearl in it, too. Mr. Toto, the owner, he's Greek, called it an attraction, said he bet his was the only gas station for miles to have something like it. He said it was

4

meant to catch attention and make people want to stop and have a look. He got the idea from South of the Border in South Carolina. Anyway, I passed the clam shell and ran straight into the store, said hey to James behind the counter. He told me to tell Aunt Di to quit sending me down there for her cigs and I nodded and paid for the cigarettes and picked out a candy bar for David and me, one each. I was about to leave when I noticed Will staring from behind a rack of Cheetos. Will is a boy from school. Quiet. Not like the other boys. I think he had some stuff going on at home that made him sad. I wanted to ask him what it was, but I didn't. What? I said and he said, Nothin. And I said, Well quit staring then. Out the door I went and ran back as quickly as I could. As I was rounding the corner, I saw the policemen getting in their car. No no no no. I needed to talk. I had questions. They weren't supposed to leave yet. The policeman saw me waving my arms like a crazy person for him to stop. He rolled down his window and smiled at me.

My heart beat so fast and I swallowed hard before I said, You gotta be straight with me. I'm not a baby. I'm eight years old. I need to know what happened. What's he done?

His smile went away. He looked down for a second and then told me to talk to my Mama about it and that everything was going to work out. Then, I cursed at him. I had never cursed at a man before but I did it then.

I said, Bullshit. Tell me what happened. You gotta tell me and not lie to me because I will know if you are lying. I am good at knowing things like that.

I heard the other officer, a woman with her hair pulled tight into a bun say, Jesus. Let's go.

The policeman looked at me, really looked me in the eye. He put the car in park and got out. I followed him to the back of the car where he leaned on the trunk. I stood in front of him with my arms crossed still catching my breath. He told me his name. I forget what it was.

Your Mama told me your name is Jo.

Yes, it is Jo. I swatted at a fly with my bag of candy and cigarettes.

That's a pretty name, Jo. And you are eight years old, Jo?

Yes sir. I am.

He nodded and scratched the back of his head.

You really ought to talk to your mama. But you seem like a smart young lady, so here's what: this is my card. See the number? You get one glimpse of your daddy, you call me. Hear me? Jo, I need to talk to him. And, I don't want him hurting y'all anymore. Can you help me?

I looked at the card. I looked at him. He smiled, patted my shoulder, then he got into the car and drove away.

Daddy came back the next day. I hid the card.

Bibba

February 5th, 2014

You listen to me, Jo. I am writing this down for you. Are you paying attention? Whatever you do from now on, you hear me. Understand? You are not this place, this beach, this house. You may look at yourself and see the girl, the terrified eight-year-old girl, the one who tried so hard to protect everyone, to be brave. You may see her and feel sorry for her or scared or angry at her. Don't, don't you do that.

You asked me what love is once. I don't remember what I said then, but I know now. Love is war. It's two people wanting things, sometimes the same things and sometimes what they want is so drastically different that it makes you wonder how they got there in the first place. Sometimes it feels like the only answer, the only way forward. There's anger and pride and propaganda for the public. There are peace talks and decisions made for the better of the people. Dining tables are set with silverware (not the good silver unless there are guests—-remember that) and paper napkins and water glasses alongside strategies and secrets. There is fighting. There are losses, gains, and moments where there is no clear winner. Most times it's worth it. Sometimes it's not.

Perhaps I'm to blame. For all of it.

2

Jo
1986

Two weeks after Daddy showed back up we celebrated
David's third birthday. I remember because Daddy had a
smile on his face and his voice was soft when he told me to
get out of the way. He looked at David. He never looked at
me that way. I don't know. Maybe he was proud. He held
David up in the air, making Mama and me nervous. He
would throw him up and catch him. David started to cry after
about the fourth time. Mama reached for my arm and
squeezed, held on to me while we watched David's small
body float up and come back down. The whole time Daddy
said to David that the girls in the house, Mama and me, were
just a couple of worthless women. And Aunt Di, too. I didn't
even know what that meant. At the time.

Thank goodness David was a heavy sleeper because I am
sure that he would not have been quiet or still like Mama told
me to be. Mama was not all big and round yet, but she was
going to have another baby. We crept out of our house that
night after we'd tied David's birthday balloon to the rocking

chair, after we cleaned up the paper plates and napkins, the candles, and wrapped up the leftover cake. We'd sneaked off like this before. Don't know how old I was, but I do remember being small, feeling small. Feeling scared. It was dark. I don't even know who picked us up. We were gone for a few days. Then, for some reason, we came back. Mama said he was going to be better, nicer. She seemed happy about it, so I guess I thought she must be right. All the times he was mean and angry and drunk and loud are mixed up in my head. But I do know that he wasn't nice for long.

Now, this time, the night of David's birthday, after Daddy was sleeping, we hurried carrying all of our things and David asleep in Mama's arms. Aunt Di was waiting in her car up the road a little bit. Through the dark, she drove us to Bibba's. Bibba is my grandmother. She smells like this perfume called RITZ, like the crackers. Not that she smells like crackers. It was just the name on the bottle. A long drive in the middle of the night? Boy, Aunt Di must be tired. She and Mama talked too low for me to hear from the backseat. David's head was in my lap. I pulled his blanket over his shoulder where it had slipped down. Aunt Di threw me a bag of donuts. She knows the ones I like, the white powdery ones. I ate those and leaned my head against the window. I had a bad feeling about leaving and I think Mama did, too.

Why'd we leave? Daddy was pushing Mama around. I saw him do it two nights before we left. He was always pushing her around, slapping at her bottom, shoving her head, but this time he seemed meaner than ever. Maybe the police coming by had him all worked up. They'd finally tracked him down and taken him to the station. Asked him all kinds of questions. He would rant about that any chance he got saying they didn't have a thing on him, they couldn't prove nothing. That night he came home late after drinking with some of his friends and Mama and him started arguing. It woke me up.

Why does everything bad happen at night? I got out of bed and crept real quiet down the hall. They were in the kitchen. I hid behind the couch. Mama was making him a sandwich, mayonnaise, ham, bread. He sat at the kitchen table, stared at her.

He said, Look at you. Fat like a hog. I could have anybody, you know. You're lucky I even look at you.

I thought that was ugly. She wasn't even hardly showing a baby belly yet. She looked real pretty in her t-shirt and pajama pants, the silky pink ones with the little blue flowers on them. Her hair long down her back. I always wanted hair like hers. Long, blonde, and soft. I thought it looked especially nice spread out on her white pillow in the morning sunshine. My hair is dark.

I wanted to run up to her and hug her and tell her she was pretty to me. But I couldn't. She just stood there with her head down. You gon' *do* something? You gon' *fight* me? He got up. He yanked a section of her beautiful hair, pulling and twisting it, turning her head to face him. She dropped the knife on the counter. I shut my eyes. I pressed my back against the living room wall. I held my breath and listened to her make whimpering sounds. I heard a click and looked. He had a gun close to her face. He grabbed her chin. Her eyes were wide. She was breathing so fast. He forced his fingers in her mouth and then put the gun in. I wanted to cry. I wanted to run in there and yell at him to stop hurting her but I was scared. I couldn't do it. My heart felt like a trapped rabbit. I was so sure he could hear it thumping. My body shook. My teeth made a t-t-tap-tap sound in my head. I put both of my hands over my mouth so he wouldn't hear me. He laughed. He *laughed* at her. Called her stupid. Then it was over. He put the gun on the table. I watched Daddy come into the room until I couldn't see him anymore. I felt him flop onto the couch. I could smell the beer he'd been drinking. I stayed quiet. I prayed I wouldn't sneeze or cough. I was afraid he would feel my body shaking. I waited and waited and waited and listened for his snoring. I don't know how long it took. It could have been an hour. Mama didn't come out of the kitchen. Once I was sure he was asleep, I slid from behind the couch. I tip-toed into the kitchen and found Mama still standing at the counter, her arms hugging her belly. She stared at the gun. I put my arms around her and she jumped. I told her it was all right, it was just me. I looked up at her face and she looked down at mine. She grabbed my shoulders. Her nails dug into my skin. She didn't look like Mama. Her face, her eyes looked wild and crazy. Then she took a breath. She held my cheeks. She started to cry. Her tears splashed onto my face.

The next day Mama said, We're going. It's a secret. Don't tell anyone. Pack your things.

When? I asked. Where are we going?

To Bibba's, she said. I sat in my room half the day trying to figure out what to take. Clothes, t-shirts and shorts, underwear, socks and shoes. I was worried that I didn't have a decent bathing suit to bring. I'd grown out of the one I used two summers ago. That's the last time I had been swimming. My toothbrush and toothpaste. I wanted to bring some sketching books and colored pencils, a sticker book, some stuffed animals and my plastic horse. I tried to fit them all in my rolly suitcase. It has wheels on the bottom and a handle that you can use to pull it along so you don't have to carry it. One of the wheels sticks, but if you give it a good yank, it will start rolling again. Mama got it from a second-hand store. It's purple with white polka dots on it. It wasn't big enough, though, for all that I wanted to take. All of my important things. Mama said I would have to choose what to leave behind. I really wanted to leave my extra clothes behind, but Mama said that wasn't a good idea and for me to hurry up and hide my suitcase when I was finished. Daddy might be home soon. That made me nervous. It felt like someone pulled a belt real tight around my stomach. I decided to leave my stickers. I was getting too old for those anyway. I packed my colored pencils and sketching books and chose my favorite stuffed animal. I would just carry my plastic horse if I didn't have space to pack it. I had to put the rest of my animals in my closet and close the door. I couldn't look at their faces.

And so, the next night, in the middle of the night, after David fell asleep, his fingers still blue from the icing on his cake, when we were all supposed to be sleeping, Mama came and got me and my suitcase. I was not asleep, though. I hadn't been able to sleep at all that night. I listened to Mama cleaning up the kitchen, washing dishes, shaking out a new garbage bag, opening and closing the refrigerator. I knew what she was doing. She was making Daddy a plate of supper. I remember that we ate meatloaf, peas and mashed potatoes that night, his favorite. Well, David didn't eat the meatloaf, but he did eat the potatoes and peas. It was just the three of us at the table. I watched Mama push the potatoes on her plate. Her fork was shaking. She looked at me and I smiled. I said, Maybe we'll get to—but she didn't let me finish. She put her finger to her lips and looked around the room like maybe he was there, maybe he could hear us. We were quiet the rest of the meal. I thought, man, Daddy was sure going to be sorry if he misses out on this food. Finally after I'd gone to bed, I heard his car in the driveway and the door slam. I counted the steps it would take for him to get to the door. One, two, three, four, five, six. The screen door creaked and the front door opened. I held my breath. I heard Mama stop the water running in the sink and then the microwave was on. I closed my eyes and prayed, He will be happy about the meatloaf, He will be in a good mood and will be happy about the meatloaf, He will be nice to her because she made him his favorite meal and that will make Him happy and full and sleepy. There was no fight that night.

I'd only been to Bibba's once. Daddy doesn't like it if we go too far. We went for one Christmas, but I don't remember much about that trip. Mama says I was three years old. I think I saw white table cloths. I remember people's shoes and being under someone's chair, a rocking chair, and Mama running over to get me. I can almost see Mama's soft skirt float as she stooped to pick me up. There was a couch covered in flowers. Dark pinks, yellows and greens. Probably all these nice things are from Bibba's house. They'd have to be because I haven't been anywhere else. I am wondering are these memories real or are they old wishes or dreams.

The car goes over a dip in the road, Aunt Di's headlights go up and down as we bounce. I finish my powdered donuts and try to picture Bibba's face. I shifted David so I could stretch out in the back of the the car. Mama told me to try and get some sleep. But I just couldn't. I watched the moon. The moon watched me. Isn't it weird how lives can be so different, but everyone looks up at the same moon? I had so much going on in my head.

I did fall asleep, though. When I woke up, everything was violet, the last color in a rainbow. The sun was coming up a little. We were driving down a long straight road that had tall trees on either side. I asked if I'd missed South of the Border and Mama said, no because we'd been driving all backroads and that's why it was taking so long. I was disappointed. That place is really tacky, but people love it. But I thank goodness I was awake to see the trees in the haze and mist. The trees seemed sad. Their branches looked droopy and old with mossy hair hanging off them. Maybe they were witches, good witches with good and happy magic. Mama said we're almost there and something about having to pee. Her voice was tired. I scooted to the middle of the long seat and watched the road to see where it was taking us. David was eating Cheerios out of a plastic bag and didn't seem to care one bit about almost being anywhere. We went over a low bridge. I could see large houses sitting near the water with docks and boats. A huge white bird with long legs stood in a shallow part of the water. I was about to say something to David about missing out on the donuts (I'm sure he could see the empty bag on the floor of the car) but then, I smelled the ocean. What a smell! I told Mama that the air around here smells so good and she smiled. Maybe she was remembering how it was to grow up there. Mama let down her window. That salty air blew all around me. I closed my eyes. My hair waved in the wind and tickled my face. We passed a grocery store called Piggly Wiggly. That made me laugh. The beach was on the left and Aunt Di pointed to a shop that was on the right called The Marina. Fishermen could bring their boats up to the marina and then go in and get snacks and fishing supplies. She explained that water on the right side led out to the bridge we just went over and the marsh where there were tall grasses growing in the water and mud and all kinds of animals and birds who liked living there. Mama nodded. We passed the elementary school and the firehouse. I got a glimpse of the ocean every few seconds as we drove past the beachfront houses. Mama spent her childhood at the beach. I've seen pictures of her and Di as little girls. Both of them in bathing suits playing in the sand. Di was making a silly face and Mama was so pretty, smiling, but not a big cheezy smile; it was a small smile and her eyes were looking off somewhere, maybe at a bird or a kite or something. I can't think of a better place to be a kid. And then, we slowed down in front of a house and turned into the driveway.

The house wasn't on the beach. It was one row back

shaded by trees and on high legs. Even though it wasn't right at the water, you could still see the ocean from the driveway. The house was butter yellow with white porch rails and brick stairs that led up to the porch. There were beautiful bushes covered in yellow flowers growing right off the porch. It was a palace. Why would Mama ever leave this place? I decided I was going to like it there.

Mama said, There she is. I looked at the house and saw Bibba coming down the porch stairs. Yes, this was where I wanted to be. Right here on Wimbee Island.

And then I thought that Daddy'd probably be waking up right about then and how he would find our beds empty and cold.

Bibba

February 18, 2014

Jo,

I need to explain things. So, I'll start over. Yes, you know my name, but I'll say it for the record: Elizabeth Ann McConnell. I was born in 1934. God, I'm old. And don't say I'm not, because I am. I am damn tired. Even as I write it down, the number looks peculiar. 1-9-3-4. It's 2014 now, a whole- nother century. Is seventy too old to start this? That's what happens to old people; we start napping in the afternoon and thinking about all we haven't said and haven't done.

I've always been "Bibba." Started with my younger brother Cal who, when he tried to say "Betty Ann," called me "Bibba" instead. It stuck, I guess. But it's not the name. That's not what I'm saying. I am not the woman Catherine and

Diana think I am despite what I am called and I've been called plenty of things. Sometimes it is hard for children to see their parents as people from before, before children. People with histories and stories. You're a mother now, so I think you'll understand. It's as if my daughters were born and they see me as if I were born at the same time, right along with them, you see? No past, no memories, just everything beginning with them. In a way, I suppose they are right. They did give me a beginning, maybe even a way to start over, but that doesn't mean my past is gone. I wish it did.

I remember the day Di called me to let me know y'all were coming.

Catherine's had enough, Mama. She can't take much more of that man. I'm getting them out. We're coming to you."

"Is that you talking, Di, or her?"

That's the way it always was with the three of us. Diana was looking out for Catherine. I was in a constant state of preparing for the next catastrophe. Catherine said one thing one day and something else the next. Her heart never could make up her mind. It worried me, especially because of you and David. Your Daddy was not a man. Ryland wasn't a husband to Catherine or a father to his children. (I know this is hard to read, Jo, but I need you to.) He wasn't human, couldn't be. Nobody does the things he did and can live with himself. And if he caught y'all leaving? I don't know. I couldn't think about it.

She'd left him before, of course, not that she had told me about it. I didn't even know until she'd already gone back. Di told me. Catherine thought I wouldn't understand, that I would give her a told-you-so speech. But that's just the thing: I know what it means to be confused, to be scared, to think you know what is best for the people you love only to realize too late how wrong you were. I've tried to tell her, but I never quite can.

The days went so slowly. I didn't know what was going on. It was too risky to try and call. So, to keep my mind on other things, I went through the house and got the rooms ready, filled the fridge, bought some buckets and shovels, you know, little toy things. I was going through some boxes I was keeping in Catherine's old room. Just a bunch of junk, really. Some old newspaper clippings, birthday cards, some dried flowers from who knows what, but then I came across a photograph I didn't realize I'd saved. Don't know why I would have kept it. It's not like it's something I want to remember.

3

I saw a dog running at my car door. Bogue! Get on back here. That's Bibba calling. I hurried up and locked the door. My mother already had her door open when this old dog ran up. Bibba walked over to the car and pulled at his neck making him get back. He had licked my entire window leaving streams of dog spit running down in front of my face. Bibba looked in my window and asked Well, are you going to get out of the car? She hugged Mama and kissed David and they smiled at each other while Aunt Di got the luggage out of the trunk. Bibba was about Mama's height, maybe a little shorter. She had blondish-white hair and blue eyes. She wore a pair of light brown pants, a white shirt with a collar, and white tennis shoes. She was pretty even though she was an old lady. Didn't wear much jewelry. A watch, a ring. Some pink lipstick.

I didn't see any men around. Mama's daddy had died when they were little girls, so Aunt Di says. Mama doesn't talk about him much.

Is that dog gone? I yelled through the window.

Jo, come on now. Mama said to me and then told Bibba that we didn't have a dog at home. Bibba squinted at me.

Everybody should have a dog, she said. I don't trust people who don't like dogs.

I unlocked the door. She opened it. I could see Bogue sitting a little ways away slobbering all over himself and waiting for me to move. He was big with short blonde-colored hair and some white on his chest. He had a big mouth and a long dangly tongue and a big black nose.

I looked at Bibba. What kind of dog is he?

She looked over at him and said, Well, Bogue is Bogue. He's just a dog, Josephine. Let's go.

I got out of the car and hugged my pillow in front of me. She closed my door. I looked up at her and said, You should call me Jo.

I grabbed my suit case handle and pulled it behind me. Mama, Aunt Di and Bibba were walking up the stairs to the front of the house. I saw Mama stop on the stairs and take a deep breath. Bibba took David from her and said, Catherine, you ought to have stopped on the way and gotten some rest.

Mama said, I'm fine.

I looked at all three women standing on the stairs and, boy, they sure did look a lot alike. All three of them had light hair and light colored eyes. People have always said that I favored Daddy. I have darker hair and brown eyes and freckles. Right then, I felt a squeeze in my stomach and wished I looked more like my Mama. I felt a wet dog nose on the back of my legs. I whimpered a little and tried scooting my suitcase in between his nose and my legs and ended up hitting him with it.

Come on now! Bibba frowned at me.

Mama said, Please don't, Mama. He just scared her. Come up here with me and David, Jo.

I pulled my suitcase up the stairs. We all went inside. I had my own room with a bed and a dresser and a closet and a table beside the bed with a lamp on it. The lamp was clear and full of sea sponges, at least that's what Mama called them. My furniture was white and the walls were white but my bedspread was yellow with pink ribbons going down in rows. So pretty! And, it had a pillow to match. Mama told me that Bibba made them, the bedspread and pillow. They were Mama's when she was little. A row of white frames hung on the wall with flowers pasted on to paper in them. They were pretty, I guess, but strange, too, all dried and the colors were yellowy. There was a window across from my bed and I could see out across the road and make out some waves in between two houses. I unpacked my clothes and put them in the dresser. I had two extra drawers, so I stuck my drawing book and colored pencils in one drawer and my toothbrush and toothpaste in the other. I had packed my stuffed rabbit and a teddy bear wearing a tuxedo. I put them on my bed and then put my plastic horse on top of my dresser. I took a step back. Looked around the room. These were all my things. All my things in the whole world. It looked good to me. I wanted to show Mama and went out into the living room to get her when I heard them in the kitchen. Bibba asked Mama had she thought about his coming here to Wimbee.

Won't this be the first place he'll look? Bibba asked.

Aunt Di said, We planned for that, Mama.

Well, my mother started saying, I don't know if it'll work, but I hid some maps of Georgia under the mattress for when he tears up the place looking for clues. And, I had you write that letter saying you were going to be visiting Aunt Alma and Uncle Cal in Virginia all summer. Not sure if he got it. He reads all my mail and never lets me see it. And, he hasn't figured out that I put by some of the grocery money for the past few months. So, I'm just praying he'll fall for it so it will give us some time. I just need some to figure things out.

Aunt Di said, Shoot, he *is* a dumbass.

David started crying.
Bibba sighed and said, We should all eat something.
I wasn't very hungry.

4

Wimbee Island is located in Colleton County, South Carolina. It was founded in the 1500s and named by some Indians. People back then grew sea island cotton and that's what made people rich, that and they owned slaves. They owned people, made them work, and treated them like dirt. I sure hoped Bibba's family hadn't done that. Then, some pesky bug came and ate it all up. That is what I learned from a book Mama was helping me read through about this beach that Bibba lives on. Bibba had this book on her shelf. She had a lot of books. There were some about history, and gardening, and a bunch of crime stories. She had a couple of shell books, too, that I wanted to take out to the beach. I picked out my favorites like the horse conchs, the angel wings, sand dollars, and olive shells. The plan was to see if I could find some of the shells from the book right out there on this Wimbee beach. Mama told me it would be hard to find the shells whole, they'd be mostly broken because of the rough ocean waters and banging on rocks, but they were still beautiful, just the same.

The very first day we arrived, I made Aunt Di take me out on the beach. Mama was tired, so she and David took a nap. I knew how much she enjoyed curling up with him, holding him close, so I didn't complain. We crossed the street and onto a small wooden walkway, then down some steps to the sand. It was sand like I'd never seen or felt before. I took my shoes off and left them on the steps. The sand was warm. I ran toward the water and stopped where the sand turned into mush. I'd never seen something so enormous. The water was as far as my eyes could see. At school I learned about how the moon pulls at the water. The waves never stop. Sometimes they are higher, faster, stronger than other times. They come in and they go out. Predictable. I liked that. Standing there, listening to the water rush onto the beach, I wondered if this was a place where people could start over, where bad things were less likely to happen and if they did or had, then you could come to the water and become someone new, someone different. I felt like I could watch the waves forever.

From what I could tell, there weren't many other kids around on Bibba's stretch of the beach. It was mostly old people walking one way and then back the other way, occasionally bending over to look at something they'd spotted in the sand. That was okay, though, because I was used to playing by myself. I was good at finding sticks and drawing in the sand. I loved going down to the beach in the morning because the sand was cool on my feet. By the afternoon, I'd have to run fast through the dry sand because it burned if I stayed on it too long. I was always on the lookout for sand dollars and sharks' teeth. By this time, I hadn't been swimming yet. Mama still needed to take me to get a new suit, and I had to wait to get a new suit before getting to swim. I was trying to be patient.

Bibba never talked directly to me much. She didn't seem like the shy type. I thought it could be that she just doesn't like kids. There are people like that, you know. It would be terrible to grow up in a house where your own mother didn't like children. Sometimes she would ask me a question or two like, how did I sleep? Or was I going to take a shower? Mama told me that she was just used to living by herself and wasn't much of a talker, so it might take a little bit for her to adjust to us. And, that I should try to stay out from under foot, especially in the kitchen. She was coming around, though. I could tell because she showed me her collection of sand dollars. She kept them in a shadowbox on the bookshelf. There were four of them, one for each person in Mama's family. Some of them were as big as my hand.

Maybe we can add one for you and one for David. What do you think?

I said, Yes, ma'am. That would be fine.

That is one other thing - Bibba was a really good cook. Not that Mama wasn't. Mama is a good cook, too, it was just different because there was just so much of it, I guess. For most of the suppers we would have a meat, a vegetable, some kind of rice or potato and a roll. David would sit there and bang his spoon on the table and I told him one time, my mouth full of *real* macaroni and cheese, that he should better go ahead and eat, we might not be eating like this for long. I remember my third night there Bibba said, I will make shrimp and grits tonight. What? I've never eaten breakfast for supper or with shrimp in it, either. But I think my favorite was the salmon patties because they tasted just like the ones Mama made and I love them with yellow mustard.

Also, I was coming around to Bogue. He sure was cute and I wanted so badly to rub my hands through his fur, but he still made me nervous whenever I went outside. I was afraid he would jump on me. I knew he wasn't a mean dog, but his teeth were long and sharp and all I could think about was him snapping out with those jaws and catching my hand. Mama showed me how to be real still and let him come up and sniff my hand. He licked it, which was okay at first but then he just kept on licking and I had to tell him to stop licking me all the time. I soon wasn't scared to go outside by myself. I knew he would be on the porch, and he would follow me there around to the side to the hammock. I wasn't allowed to go off the porch by myself, so I went out to the hammock mostly to look at books or use Bibba's binoculars to watch the seagulls. Seagulls are pesky. Don't ever eat your peanut butter and jelly sandwich out where the seagulls can see you. They will fly up to the porch and pace on the railing and look at you sideways wanting a piece of your sandwich. Bibba told me not to give them any because then they will just keep on coming back. That was what Bogue was good for. He didn't like the seagulls either. He chased them off the porch. I gave him part of my sandwich to say thanks. Also, Bogue liked corn chips just about as much as me.

Aunt Di was only supposed to stay a couple of days. She had to get back to her office manager job at the storage place. And she had to drive five and half hours back to Lenoir, NC by herself. But at the last minute she decided not to go. Who would want to leave the beach? Bibba called it *wise*. They needed to figure things out first. Aunt Di said Billy, her manager at the storage place, would understand. Billy was in love with Aunt Di, and that's a fact. As much as I don't understand everything about Aunt Di, she is funny and pretty, too. I think she should marry Billy. He's nice and calm and gives me candy.

Did I ever tell you I am originally from Lenoir? We have mountains and forests and long curving roads that go up and up and up, which is a lot different from the beach. Bibba called me a yankee girl for living in North Carolina instead of South Carolina like she does. I asked Mama why we didn't live in South Carolina. She told me that Daddy had moved them up here after they got married. He had a cousin in

Lenoir that got him some work with a furniture company. Aunt Di had just finished high school and decided to move up here, too, which made Mama happy because they are the best of sisters. I can't see how they are. Di is always picking at Mama. Mama is always rolling her eyes at Di. Mama says Di doesn't tease her to be ugly. She tells me not to be so suspicious of everyone. Aunt Di has been working at that storage place ever since they moved up to Lenoir. I think Aunt Di likes Mama a lot more than she says she does, just for the record.

I got used to Bibba's house, too. I went around and counted four bedrooms, a living room with a TV, two bathrooms with showers, a kitchen with a table in it, a porch that went almost all the way around the house and a place to park the cars underneath. She had locks on all the doors and windows. Plus a storage shed and an outdoor shower. Mama told me that you weren't supposed to get naked in that shower. It was just for washing sand off when you come up from the beach. I thought why on earth would I get naked outside anyway and the water to that shower was way too cold. Oh, and on the mailbox there was a sign that said: DOC'S DOCK. My grandfather was a doctor and he put up that sign. You could walk up some steps and out in front of the house and follow a path to cross the street and to the beach. It was that close! And there were hardly ever that many cars driving down the street to watch out for. Bogue wouldn't go with you unless you called him, which I thought was pretty good behavior. Aunt Di followed me and Bogue down there a few times and watched me throw sticks. That dog would go and get those sticks and bring them back for me to throw over and over again. I would get tired of that and have to tell him I am done playing with you right now.

Finally, Mama took me to the grocery store, the only grocery store on the island and bought me a new bathing suit. They have a whole aisle of beach stuff like towels and bathing suits and sunscreen and chairs and coolers. My suit is green with little pink fish on it and straps that criss-cross in the back. I also got a towel that is bigger than I am, and it is blue with a big yellow sun on it and it says, Sun is Fun. Mama also picked up some sunscreen, which I hate putting on, but she makes me and says I can't go out to the beach unless I am wearing some. She tells me that I will thank her when I'm older, but I don't think so. It stinks and makes me feel greasy and takes forever for Mama to put it on me. David hates it even more than I do and he was always pulling off his sun hat. I was willing to put up with it, though, if it meant I got to go play on the beach.

There was something about being on the beach. It made me want to fly. The wind, the bright beautiful blue sky. I could just take off running and lift into the air over the water and wave at Mama and Bibba. They'd both yell to not go too high. Bogue would bark and want to fly with me. I'd close my eyes and feel the hot sun and then swoosh down close to the water like the pelicans. I'd dip my fingers in the water and zoom back into the sky. But I would always fly close to the house. I'd never get lost.

Bibba had a big old faded blue umbrella. She would dig a hole and put the end of the umbrella in the sand and bury it. It stayed up pretty good unless there was a lot of wind and then we would have to go inside. I made sandcastles and collected shells in my bucket. David ate sand. David cried. He rubbed his sandy hands all over his face. I love my little brother, but he sure can be a handful sometimes. Bibba had floaties she said I had to wear if I wanted to go in the ocean. I looked at Mama and she nodded. I turned around and looked at that wide ocean and the waves coming in on the sand and thought, yeah, I could probably use some help, but not for long. Mama walked out with me, holding my hand. She

27

warned me about rip tides and how I could get pulled out and no matter how hard I swam, it would be too hard for me to get back to the beach, so I had to be careful not to get caught up in one. She was wearing a bathing suit, too, except she had some shorts on with it. She said she didn't like taking them off. I told her that was fine. We walked into the mushy part of the sand. The part where the water would rush up on you and squished my toes down until they disappeared. We laughed and then Mama showed me how to jump over the waves as they were coming in. I lost a shovel in the ocean.

Aunt Di and Bibba did not wear bathing suits down to the beach. Aunt Di wore shorts and t-shirts and Bibba wore her khakis rolled up and fancy t-shirts with lacy or beaded designs on them, and, of course, her pink lipstick. They both stayed under the umbrella, read books, looked through the binoculars at shrimp boats or just watched people walk by. Some stopped to talk and Bibba would point at me and Mama and Di and I knew she was telling them we were visiting. Sometimes Bibba didn't come down to the beach at all. She would stay and do house stuff. No fun! Aunt Di and Mama and me would pick up our things and head back to the house and find Bibba fixing lunch while David napped on Mama's bed. Sometimes she talked on the phone or read the newspaper or made notes in her notebook. Sometimes she went down to the shops at the pier to visit some friends. She knew Miss Nadine, the lady who owned the gift shop. I went with Mama to the shop and Miss Nadine grabbed Mama in a bear hug. She was wearing a bright yellow, flowy, silky-looking shirt and white pants. She had a big chest, her bosom I mean, which made her look large, but she had little bird legs and I wondered how she didn't fall right over. Her short hair was styled up and pointy almost like spikes and it was a definite color job. It was just so blonde. I couldn't stop staring. Her fingernails were long, probably fake, painted hot pink, and scratched my face when she grabbed my chin. Miss Nadine said, Are you Jo? She got close to my face and I could see all the make-up she was wearing, thick in the creases of her face; her blue eyeliner was smudged. I liked her shell earrings, though. They were pretty. Her store was real nice, too. Mama let me go walk through the store. I turned the rack of keychains looking for one with my name, but it wasn't there. I tried on some flip-flops and sunglasses. I went around past the folded t-shirts and started looking through the beach toys and listened to Miss Nadine.

It's so nice you've come to visit. It's been awhile, hadn't it?

Yes. Mama's voice was low and soft.

Well, I guess Wimbee hasn't changed all that much since you were last here. Everything's just chugging right along. Just the five of you up at the house?

That's right.

I suppose Ryland couldn't get off work? To join ya'll on your visit?

I froze because Ryland is my Daddy and I had not been thinking about him the past few days and then I was suddenly thinking about him and wondering what she knew about him and why she was asking. I took off the hat and sunglasses not knowing what to do with them, so I dropped them on the floor. All I wanted was to leave. I grabbed Mama's hand. Mama said that she was right, he couldn't come because of work. Miss Nadine just smiled and said, Well, I hope y'all will come by as often as you like. And I was thinking that I would not like to come by very often. We left and I asked Mama why that woman was so nosy and Mama told me not to think bad things about her, that she *was* nosy, but that it wasn't her fault. God made her that way to show little girls like me how *not* to behave. Mama told me before not to ask grownups what they do for a living or to talk about money. After we left the shop, she added to this list not to ask where a woman's husband was.

Bibba

April 22, 2014

I need you to stick with me here, Jo. All of this is important.

You know the old Presbyterian Church on the island. It's been there for hundreds of years. Some of the headstones in the cemetery go back to the 1700s. Robertson, Peavy, Dowling, just some of the names you'll find there. And, of course, Shields, my maiden name. We have a long history here. I know every tree that shades the picnic tables on the lawn outside the church. I've helped line the front steps with lilies for many Easter Sundays and poinsettias for Christmas. I was married there. Your Mama and Aunt Di were baptized, their souls washed of sin by a handful of water from the church's font which, if you were to take a few steps outside, is mere feet from a marsh and a mile or so from the ocean's edge that somewhere through stretches of deep sea and slow leaking lakes in high mountains and shallow valley streams and creek beds is connected to the River Jordan. And so are the souls of my children; therefore, so are you.

When I look at the picture I found in the box I see a nineteen year old me (this was back in 1953) leaning against the rail fence that separated the gravel parking lot from the church's lawn. My white blouse is tucked into the high waist of my skirt. The skirt is long, mid-calf length, nothing like the skirts girls wear today. Proper, modest. Just the way Mother liked it. There is, if I work to see it, squinting my eyes and filling in the blanks with what I remember, a brooch pinned on my blouse's crisp collar. It was gold-colored metal shaped into three lily blooms, their stems held together with a bow. At the center of the bow was a single pearl. *My pearl*, my father used to call me. The brooch was a present for my sixteenth birthday.

The bright hot sun beat down that day, but I can't remember the feel of it or smell the freshly shucked oysters that were roasting for the July Fourth picnic. I look past that girl who looks like me, whose carefree face is turned up to the shining sun because she doesn't know what is about to happen. I look at the girl I think was me to what I know is there past the ladies serving strawberry pies and peach cobblers, past the Deacons smoking their pipes, past the tables and the lawn chairs, the blur of children chasing each other. Far from the crowd, a smudge on the photo paper, a stain? No, a group of boys standing by an oak tree.

I know I don't talk about your grandfather much. There's a reason for everything and I hope that by telling this story to you, I can help you (and maybe me) understand. For some reason it's just easier to write it down than to say it out loud. Does that make sense?

I was waiting until Mother said it was all right for Connie to walk me down to the pier. I longed to walk with him away from everyone's eyes and ears. Even our friends watched us, waiting for the fault in our relationship to show. People were envious. I twirled around, my skirt swinging out brushing against Connie's neatly pressed pants. He smiled and rested his hands on my elbows pulling me in. Just a hint of my jasmine perfume. I pulled back and he let my arms slide through his rough hands until he was holding mine, not wanting me to go.

"I forgot my sheet music and Dr. Long will kill me if I don't have it for rehearsal tomorrow. Wait for me, Connie?"

"For you? Forever."

He was like that. Like out of a movie. I am smiling remembering him like this. A gentleman caller with passion in his eyes and a pressing heat in his hands. We were young and in love. He was a medical student in Charleston, home for a visit and we were desperate to be together.

The group of boys by the oak tree had moved over to one of the cars parked on the road. Connie looked over at them. There were three, two tall and one shorter, stockier than the other two. I recognized the two tall boys as the Perry twins, the pastor's boys. The third wasn't from Wimbee that I knew. Always up to no good. They were laughing and making rude gestures that were meant for us. The stocky one stood and grinned. Connie said, "Don't pay them any mind." And so I didn't. We were saving ourselves from ourselves. I had thoughts and imaginings fueled by whispered stories and presumptions from some girlfriends. I couldn't be sure what Connie thought as we linked fingers, blushed, and promised to wait, promised to be with each other. Promised the world. *Yes, John Matthew McConnell, my Connie, I promise to wait for you.*

The air in the sanctuary was hot and tight, hard to breathe. The service ended almost an hour before, but I remember the oppressive air in the room even with its high ceiling and white walls and worn wooden pews, the wooden floors, all of it seemed layered with the smell of sweat, as if everyone had just left. But it wasn't true. It had been almost an hour. The food had been blessed and lunch was well underway. Families were together, brothers and sisters, mothers and fathers. Friends. Neighbors. People passing plates and sharing words and sharing space. It was all intimate, really. In the sanctuary, I was alone.

I walked past the wooden stairs to the lectern and stepped on to the deep red carpet loft. This was a place I'd felt most myself. During a service, I would watch the back of Pastor Perry's head as he gave his sermon, his arms floating up and down or his hands pointing up depending on his inflection. If I looked out into the congregation, I ran the risk of catching my brother Cal's eye and he would stick out his tongue and make me laugh. Mother would be horrified. I stared at Pastor Perry's robes or the bald spot on the back of his head trying to keep my mind on his words. When it came time to sing, I felt my heart swell with anticipation. I loved it, Jo, truly. I was good a singer, not great, but good. It was the way the songs made me feel. I felt such a connection to God, to the church, to the people, when I sang.

There were three rows of wooden chairs. I touched the back of the first chair as I stepped up to the next row, my row. Second row, third seat from the end. I saw the white papers beneath my chair and felt relief. I hadn't lost my music.

I am trying, Jo, but I have to stop.

5

Jo
1986

I was watching TV when the phone rang. It was Billy for Aunt Di. Aunt Di was in the kitchen on the phone and I heard her say Billy's name and asking things like when and what did you say. Mama got up from the table where she was wiping applesauce from David's mouth and walked over to Aunt Di. That's when I knew. I could tell by looking at her face. She caught me looking at her and she smiled and waved and I looked back at the TV But I had already seen that episode, so I listened real close to Mama and Aunt Di talking in the kitchen. Turned out Daddy came by the storage place asking questions. Billy told Daddy that Aunt Di had gone to Cherokee with some friends to do some gambling and that he wasn't sure when she'd be back. He said Daddy looked like he didn't believe him and that Daddy told him okay I know where to find you if I got more questions. Daddy was looking for us.

That night a noise woke me up. It was so dark. There was someone in the hallway. I don't know why I got up. I couldn't breathe. Didn't want to breathe. Didn't want to make a sound. What if it was him? Was he out there? I put my ear to the door and then, I don't know what made me open it. Maybe, somehow I just knew Mama was in trouble. I saw someone in the darkness. It was Bibba. She had a ball of sheets in her arms. Aunt Di was leaning against the wall with David who was still asleep in her arms. Di had her head down, rubbing her cheek back and forth on the top of David's head. Bibba was whispering something to her and then I heard Mama crying. I wanted to go to her but I didn't know what was going on. I got back in bed and pulled the sheets over my head.

In the morning I was hopeful I'd had a bad dream. Everything was quiet like the house was still sleeping. I could hear the waves and the cries of the birds down at the beach. I stood in front of my door for a while and stared at my toes. I counted them from left to right and then right to left. I didn't hear anyone talking. I didn't hear anyone doing anything. The only sound was the waves on the beach. And the birds calling and crying. I opened my door and looked down the hall. Mama's door was closed. I went into the living room, but there wasn't anyone there. I looked in the kitchen. The light was on and I could smell coffee. I walked to the screen door that went out on the porch. I saw Bibba in the rocking chair with the cup she held pressed to her chest under her chin. David was sitting at her feet pushing pine straw through the spaces between the porch planks. Her eyes were fixed out across the street. Bogue was lying at the steps. He looked up at me and wagged his tail.

Bibba said, Come out here, Jo.

She hadn't even looked at me. I pushed open the door and walked out on the porch. I waited.

She said, Come over here where I can see you. Bogue did not move. I faced her.

Your mama isn't feeling well today. She was sick last night. But she'll be all right. I'm taking her to my doctor today. Your aunt will stay here with you.

I bit my lip. Was she done talking? I want to see her, I said.

She's sleeping, she said.

What is she sick with?

I don't want you worrying about that. She's going to be okay.

I just want to look at her.

There was something about Bibba's face. Her cheeks were hanging low, like her skin was falling forward more than ever. She was still beautiful to me, but sad, tired. I wondered if everything was catching up to her. I knew it was a lot having all of us living with her.

You can see her, but don't wake her.

She took me inside and down the hall. We opened Mama's door quietly and I looked in. Her back was to us and before Bibba could catch me, I made it over to the other side of the bed. I bent down and put my chin on the mattress. Our noses touched.

I knew you weren't sleeping, Mama, I whispered.

Tears were coming down my face. They ran onto her nose and down soaking into the sheet. I could smell her breath, but I didn't care. I touched her cheek. She looked at me and all I wanted was to climb in with her. I wanted her to wrap her arms around me and fit my head into the curve of her neck, like we sometimes do.

She said, Don't cry, Jo. The baby is gone now, but don't you cry. She shut her eyes and Bibba took me by the shoulder and led me out. Bibba and I sat outside her door. She held my face and I cried until I was done.

Bibba

May 12th, 2014

I'm sorry about my handwriting. This part is hard for me, but I'm going to finish it this time. I thought the church was empty. Everyone outside. I reached for my sheet music. When he put his hand over my mouth and pushed me down on my knees, it didn't make any sense. Had I fallen? Tripped? He must have been trying to catch me, to keep me from falling. It was an accident. He didn't mean to grab my face or push me down. I sucked in air and felt his hand over my lips. I could taste them. I grabbed at his fingers to loosen his grip. It was only a second or two from the time he came up behind me to the time I was on my knees that these things flew through my head because the reality of what was happening was unthinkable. He couldn't be pushing my face into the deep red carpet. He couldn't be forcing my skirt up, ripping my underwear down. It just couldn't be real.

He told me me to be quiet.

Don't make a sound. I can tell you want it.

There's a hymn. O'God This Night. It came to me, just this one part and I sang it silently as a prayer over and over again.

O' God this night, thy face is near
Through shades of darkness, your presence here
With weary arms, I cast my sins upon your sea
And the tempest passes o'er me
I close my eyes and find restful sleep

I lay there and lay there, not sure if he was gone. Not sure if I could move. It was over or maybe it was still happening. I stared at the red carpet and realized I was on my side, curled up. I heard something. A door. A voice. Laughter? No. Who would laugh? Footsteps. Close. I drew my legs up to my chest and covered my face with my hands.

There was a tunnel. Hollow voices reverberated off dark walls. Sounds, maybe words bounced from one ear to the other. My name, Bibba. *Bibba Bibba I'm so sorry Bibba*, multiplied and floated. My name. Then there was a light in the mad darkness. I was looking at Connie. I realized I was looking at Connie. It was his voice I heard and his hands brushing the hair out of my face. I should've been grateful to see him. His eyes were fretful and searching. I should've been relieved to hear his rapid breath. But I wasn't. I wanted to die.

Mother was in agony and couldn't keep any food down. She became thin and twitchy, nervous at every sound. Daddy's heart had been broken since he returned from the war and now it was shattered into a thousand slivers, tiny and sharp and scattered, never able to put it back right. Lord, this is only coming to me now, as I write this down: because he was in pieces, he wanted to break other things, a crystal vase knocked off a shelf, a mirror flung to the floor, all things in shards. Because without the chaos, if it were all to stop, if he let in the silence, he'd have to stare at his little girl, at me, his pearl, and feel nothing but shame. My poor Daddy.

Mother put up with his anger and hid her grandmother's tea service. I watched her try to eat toast while holding my hand. Just the way she had pressed my hand in hers that day, not wanting to let me go, when I wasn't sure if I ever wanted to be touched again. My younger brother Cal stalked the hallways and stood guard on the front porch, tearing the leaves off Mother's gardenia bushes, ripping them into tiny pieces. He was hot with anger, as young men can be, and didn't know what to do with himself. Mother had to beg him to go back to school.

And then there was Connie. I'd told him to wait while I found my music that horrible day. He'd waited outside by the fence until he decided he'd waited long enough. The afternoon was passing and his visit was coming to an end. He wanted more time with me. He'd had enough of the gentlemen talk and hoped we could go on a walk together before it got too late. He went inside the church to find me. He saw my shoe first. It had come loose and fallen down the dark red carpeted steps. Like Cinderella's glass slipper except, to say it plainly, she hadn't been raped and left bleeding on the carpet in the sanctuary of the church, a place she'd loved. She hadn't lain, and focused on the words of her favorite hymn. She hadn't closed her eyes and silently sung allowing the darkness to close around her heart.

I cast my sins upon your sea
And the tempest passes o'er me

It's all too familiar that small towns have big mouths. Everyone knew something had happened. Mother wouldn't allow Daddy to ask about it. I sat at my desk in my room and watched through sheer curtains as cars drove slowly up the dirt drive to the house. The Sheriff came and asked Daddy questions. Mother begged Daddy not to say anything. I saw girlfriends and their mothers walking up our steps carrying covered dishes. Mother told them how kind they were and that I was really fine, just had a scare in the dark sanctuary or had tripped trying to reach for my music, that's all and told them to say hello to their husbands and fathers for us.

I stayed home even after my body healed and wandered about the house as if to find something missing. I crept into the quiet rooms to hide, my feet bare so I wouldn't make a sound. I didn't want anyone to find me, to look at me, to speak to me. I wanted the silence, the solitude. It felt like all I could handle or deserved. I ran my fingers over the gold letters on book bindings in the library. I closed the cover on the piano and tucked my sheet music in the bench. At night, I lay in bed and listened to the evening summer storms build over the ocean and come to shore, thunder and lightning and salty wind. I remembered the smell of his breath, a sweet stench mixed with cigarettes. His hands were on my mouth, in my clothes, on my body, pulling and twisting. The power in his thrust ripped me apart shooting pain through every nerve. Two of my fingernails broke while I was digging in the carpet, looking for something to hold on to. He pulled out and spit on his hands and then went again. That's when I shut my eyes tight and held my breath. My mind went to my song. I saw the music in my head, followed the notes and repeated the words as a silent plea.

Was it real? Yes. Oh, God, yes.

What did he take from me? And what had he left in its place?

6

Jo
1986

Mama lost the baby exactly one month after we had arrived at Bibba's. I don't always understand the words grownups use. She didn't *lose* the baby. She didn't forget where she put it like a barrette or a wallet. It wasn't her fault. The baby just died, is all. While Bibba took Mama to the doctor, Aunt Di sat me down and asked me if I knew what was going on. I almost started crying again and shook my head no. Your mother started bleeding last night. Sometimes it happens. I stared at her. She said the baby was still pretty small and I guess it just wasn't strong enough, so, well, it died. We sat there for a minute or two and she asked if I understood.

Is Mama was going to be okay? I asked.

Yes, but it might take a while for her to get back to normal. She might be sad for a little while, but that is typical. Don't go and bother her about it.

She patted my knee and told me to get on out of the kitchen because she needed to do some cleaning. I thought knowing what happened would make me feel better.

It didn't.

I promised not to bother her or ask for anything. I hung out with Bogue until Bibba brought Mama home. Mama smiled at me and asked me how my morning had been. I said fine and she said good and went on in the house to lie down. She stayed in her room for two whole days. I had a hard time keeping myself busy. David was crying all the time and I kept trying to come up with games to play with him. I let him take my markers and colored pencils. He mashed them all over the paper drawing who knows what, broke the tips, used yellow and black together, ruining my yellow marker. I watched TV and looked through Bibba's photo album she kept on the bookshelf. For some reason it felt like something I shouldn't be doing, like I'd get in trouble, so I waited until everyone else was busy. I grabbed the album and went out on the steps with it. It was big and brown and had plastic sheets you could pull back to put the photos on the paper or take them out, if you wanted. Some were in black and white and some in color. I liked the color ones best, even though they were faded. I could see Mama's gold hair shinning in the sun. That's the first time I ever saw a picture of my grandaddy. He was tall and handsome. I remember thinking that everyone in the pictures was pretty. Granddaddy wore glasses and had a nice face. In one picture he is sitting with Mama and Aunt Di on his lap, his long arms wrapped around them. Aunt Di was looking up at him and has the biggest smile on her face. I don't know. I'd never seen her look like that before, like a little girl, even younger than me. Mama was a little bigger and smiling at the camera, a few teeth missing, her hand is blurry from waving.

I turned the page and saw older pictures, black and white ones. I realized that I was looking at Bibba in her wedding gown and Granddaddy in his suit and tie. He looks happy and I guess she does, too, except she isn't looking at the camera. Her eyes are looking off to the side.

Bibba and Aunt Di wouldn't let me go down to the beach by myself, so I always had to wait on one of them to go with me. I liked it better when Mama went with me. You know what? I think Bibba and Aunt Di are exactly alike. They didn't talk to me much and when they did, it was mostly bossy. Bibba told me to take the hose and spray the sand off the walkway and I didn't want to because my show was coming on and she said, Jo, you better get your fanny out there and wash off that walkway or I'm going to get after your behind with this fly swatter.

Aunt Di was always on me about making up my bed and putting my dishes in the dishwasher and telling me that she wasn't my maid. Well, I didn't think she was my maid. I just didn't care about my bed being made up, especially since I was going to be getting back in it later and Mama always took my dishes from me at our house.

But this wasn't our house. This wasn't my room or my bed.

I got worried. I started to wonder about school starting up in September. How was I going to get back for school? When were we going to go buy school supplies, and how would I find out who my teacher was? Do we have to go home? This made me even more nervous. I couldn't think of a way to go home, back to school without Daddy finding out. We just can't go home. Maybe we were going to stay with Bibba. What school would I go to here? Do kids go to school on this island? How do they stand being stuck in school when the beach is right out there? And, I realized that my shorts were getting too tight.

I need to go to the store, I said.

Bibba looked over the top of her glasses. The lenses were all fogged up. She was standing, stirring a pot of steaming water. She was cooking rice. I watched the clouds over her eyes shrink, but not wanting them to. I didn't want to look in her eyes.

Why, she asked.

Well, my shorts are uncomfortable and I need a new pair.

She looked at me and nodded. Okay, I think you're probably right. I'll take you tomorrow.

I don't have any money, I said biting some loose skin on my thumb.

Bibba rested her wooden spoon across the top of the pot.

That's okay. We'll work it out. And quit biting those nails.

The next day, Bibba drove me all the way off the island to a department store called White's. This was the first time I rode in her car. It was a 1986 Cadillac. She called it Cotillion White with brown seats. It was huge! I sat in the front on my knees so I could see out the window on my side. It was like going through a green tunnel. The trees all lined up so close to the road, like someone just drove a train through the middle of them, making a road for people to travel on. We passed the old post office, fresh food stands, kids kicking rocks. It was weird at first, riding in the car with her. I didn't know if I should say something. I played with the ash tray cover on my door, open and close and open and close, but then she turned on the radio and let me choose a station. I couldn't believe that. That was pretty nice. Aunt Di never lets me choose. I settled on a station that was playing a song I know. I know it because it was a song Mama loves to sing. I don't remember the name of it or who sings it. It's an old song. Bibba started singing and I sang with her:

There's a scene I keep playing in my mind.
The ocean waves and moonlight shimmering,
And it's you and me that night.
But all that's left is the memory.

* * *

Mama would always sing and bounce in her seat and it made me so happy to watch her. Bibba didn't sing quite as loud, but she was smiling and she was happy. That was enough for me.

On the way home, Bibba pulled up a dirt road. There was a big white sign with fancy black letters that read "Shields House" and Bibba explained that this was where she'd grown up. Where she'd grown up? I looked out across the gigantic yard, green with grass, that led up to a large white house and black shutters on the windows and tall columns on the front porch and long tan-colored fields spread out behind and beside the house.

Bibba's old house. Wow.

These oak trees you see have been here for as long as the island has been around. I used to climb them like you do now.

She smiled at me. And, I was wearing dresses doing it. Can you imagine?

When she remembers things, it's like she is younger. She looked happy talking about her childhood.

My brother Cal and I would race up the road, our nice clothes dusty by the time we go to the house. Mother never liked that. And Daddy would be out in those fields working with other men.

Why don't you live here now? I asked.

Now? Well, because I got married and was supposed to live with my husband in a new house, have my own family. My parents lived here until they died. Cal and I sold it. My brother Cal. Your great-uncle. It's a historical property now. A bed and breakfast. And there's a golf resort on the other side of the property. Can't see it from here.

Bibba turned around in the driveway and started back down the road. This place is a part of you, too, you know. A part of your history. You didn't just begin in Lenoir. There's a lot that happened before Lenoir that helps to make you who you are.

I turned around in my seat and watched the house get smaller and smaller as we rode away.

It was evening when we returned to Bibba's house. Mama was up in the living room sitting in a chair and drinking tea. I rushed over to her and hugged her. Aunt Di yelled at me to not be so rough but I didn't care and Mama hugged me back and smiled. I asked her how she was feeling and she said she was better and wanted to know what was in my bags. I put on a fashion show for her while David played on the floor, not giving one flip about my new clothes. Bibba got me four new pairs of shorts, a pair of new shoes and some shirts. I could mix and match the shirts with the shorts to make different outfits. I liked that. I figured that meant less time trying to figure out what to put on in the morning. I remember I was the happiest I had felt in days with Mama up and some new things to look at. Also, we had banana pudding that night to celebrate Mama's feeling better.

It took a few days to get Mama out and about. She finally walked down to the beach with me and Bogue. Bogue was so happy to run around just like how I felt. I think we'd both been a little cramped up in the house. Mama wore a smile the whole day and for a while she even threw a ball for Bogue. I noticed her taking a lot of deep breaths and I asked her if she needed to go back in.

No, Jo. I'm fine. It's just the air out here. It smells good. Her arms were wrapped around her body. She was giving herself a hug. I gave her a hug, too.

Yes, I said, It does.

7

Aunt Di was on the porch when we came back from the beach. It was almost time for my show to come on and it was downright hot out, so we decided to go in to cool off. Di spotted us and smiled. When we reached the porch Mama asked what was wrong.

Nothing, everything is fine. I did hear from Billy a little bit ago. She swayed from side to side stretching her back. Her ash tray was full of stinky cigarette butts, so she must have been waiting for a while.

Mama stopped and looked at her. Go on in, Jo. I'll be in in a minute. You don't want to miss your show, now. She was right. I didn't want to miss my show, but I could tell something fishy was going on. I did what I was told but kept an ear out for any problems. They were out there for a while. I started to not feel so good, like maybe I was going to throw up. But I didn't want to tell anybody. I didn't want to be treated like a baby. My heart was racing. I wanted to know the truth. I rubbed my hands back and forth on the carpet. The lump in my throat was growing. Just as the star of my show was singing her goodbye song they came in from the porch. Mama looked all right. I guess I half expected her to be upset and sick again. She smiled at me and said everything was fine. I got up and went to her.

Is it Daddy? Is he coming for us? Did he find us? I was really serious and I couldn't keep the words from flying out of my mouth.

Mama sat down and told me to sit with her. I want you to understand something. I will never let him hurt you, do you understand? We're going to be just fine, okay? Now, what else are you worried about? She stroked my hair.

I wanted to believe her. I couldn't slow my breathing.

You know how someone asks you a question and you can hold it all in except when your Mama asks you a question and you're worried about things, you just can't hold it? That's how it was at that moment. If anyone else had asked me what I was worried about, I would have been able to keep it all together, but because she smelled like her and she looked like her and she was warm and safe, I started to cry and talk at the same time about Daddy and school and the baby and her getting sick again. Bibba stepped over and told me to put my head between my legs to calm me down. It helped. Mama wiped my hair off my face and hugged me until I felt better. Once I was able I asked her to be honest and tell me what Billy was calling about. She took a deep breath and turned me to face her.

Your Daddy ended up in jail last night because of his drinking. Got into some fight at a bar over, nothing, probably. Sounds like he really messed up this time. He called Billy this morning to pick him up from the police station and take him home. Billy said that Daddy was crying the whole way home about us being gone and that he seemed really sorry and sad. What else would you like to know?

I wanted to know how I was going to go to school. She told

me not to worry that I wouldn't miss any school and how would I like to go to school here and make some new friends? She had all she needed to sign me up. She could go fill out all the paperwork next week. I thought that sounded fair. So I took a deep breath and blew my nose and went to wash my face and lie down for a bit.

I hoped Daddy wasn't too sad. And if I'm telling the truth, I didn't miss him that much. I hoped Mama didn't miss him much, either.

A couple of days later Mama and I were at the grocery store when a man approached us. I was immediately anxious about the man. Mama told me it was okay because he was on old friend of hers. He was very smiley and wiped his hands on his pants before shaking her hand. I think he held her it a little too long, if you ask me. I looked in his buggy and didn't see any beer. That was good. I did see some ice cream and a frozen pizza. That was a lot better than our buggy. All we had so far was some broccoli and a loaf of bread.

His name was Hetch. I thought that was funny. I'd never heard that kind of name before. Mama explained that it was a nickname. His last name was Hetchings and his first name was Thomas, but everybody called him Hetch because his father was named Thomas, too. I do see how that could be confusing.

When we got home Bibba asked, Catherine, what is going on?

Mama looked surprised and wanted to know what she meant.

Bibba said, I am your mother and I know something is up. I can tell by looking at you.

I looked at Mama to see if I could see what Bibba was talking about. And you know what? I could. Her face was shining and her cheeks were pink. Mama's mouth twisted up and she fanned herself with the grocery receipt.

Mama saw a friend, that's all, Bibba, I said heaving a bag of baking potatoes onto the counter. Bibba wanted to know who and when Mama told her Hetch, Bibba threw down her kitchen towel and said she was going to fold laundry. Mama bent over and covered David's head and face with kisses. He reached for her. She took David out of his high chair where Bibba had strapped him while he ate some crackers.

She doesn't like Hetch? I asked Mama.

Well, Hetch and I used to date some in high school. He was a few grades above me. His daddy was a real nice man and your Bibba got along with his mother real well, too. But, we had to stop seeing each other.

Why, was he ugly to you?

Mama rubbed my cheek and said, No, honey. She sat me on the couch and told me their story. She said:

Hetch was dating a girl before he dated me. It'd been over for a few months when we started dating. He was a couple of years ahead of me in school, a senior. He was on the baseball team, played second base, real quick on his feet. A good arm, too. He was tall and lanky and had bushy light brown hair that stuck out all over the place when he took his cap off. He came up to me after a game. It was a shut-out, a quick nine innings. Our team won. I was waiting for Bibba to come get me. Introduced himself and offered to wait with me. It was getting dark and my girlfriends were already gone. I was a suspicious at first. Why was he talking to me? I didn't feel all that interesting. We sat and talked about all kinds of things, our families, friends, school, until Bibba showed up. I remember feeling sorry to see her car. I wanted another minute with him. I wanted to hear his voice a little longer,

51

watch him toss his baseball and catch it in his glove like it was a natural thing. He asked if he could see me again. Bibba liked him and was okay with it. We were together after that, it seems. We fell in love pretty quickly. Too quickly. But, love has its own ideas. Anyway, a few months later he came to me and told me, well, he told me that his old girlfriend was going to have a baby. And he felt like he had to do the right thing and marry her. I was so upset. Angry, really. How could he have gotten himself in that situation? But, Jo, at the root of anger is always heartache and hurt. And that's what I really was, heartbroken. I had a lot of plans, a lot of dreams, all of them involving Hetch and me together. I think it scared me, too, because I wasn't the kind of girl to get pregnant like that, which made me think that he wished I was, or would want me to go that far with him. I don't know. I wasn't ready for all that. I didn't realize that he was. And the real shame of it all is that the girl ran off with some other guy before the wedding. I don't know if Hetch ever saw the baby.

I thought for a minute, not really understanding and said, But why didn't y'all get back together?

Mama sighed and said, Bibba wouldn't allow it. I wasn't supposed to talk to him or see him. Your grandmother wanted the best for me. Mama looked at me and I felt sorry for her. She rubbed my back and said, Honey, I'm not even sure what I wanted. I was confused. I knew I loved him and he was trying to do the right thing...

Mama was struggling to find the right words.

I couldn't understand it. Who was this man that Mama had loved? Who was she when she loved him? It was a life unfamiliar to me, had never heard about, thought about.

I asked, How did you know? That you loved him?

I think it's different from one person to the next, honey. It's not always what you see on TV All sweet music, dreamy eyes, and romance every second. I remember he made me feel excited and also calm at the same time. I remember holding his hand and thinking how perfectly made for mine it was. I remember looking at him and knowing that he needed me. Jo, love isn't simple. Love is a lesson. And like most things that are supposed to teach us something, it's much easier to see the lesson in hind-sight. If you listen, love can tell you who you are.

Did he break your heart, Mama? Cause if he did, I will not like him.

Jo, he probably did break it a little back then, but he's a man now. It seems foolish to hold it against him.

Aunt Di walked in and asked what else Mama would like to hold against him. Mama got all red in the face and she told Di to hush. Di said, Ha! And Mama ushered me out of the kitchen.

Here is something that I know: My mother is very beautiful. Men like her. She is always getting compliments when we are out running errands or doing things. It embarrasses her, but there is nothing she can do about it. Hetch was no surprise to me at all.

8

The middle of July snuck up on us. It was all going so fast. Mama was much better. She seemed a lot happier and even went out shopping by herself a few times, something she hadn't done since we arrived at Bibba's. Hetch had come around a couple of times, too. I suspected something. I wasn't quite sure what was going on, but something was happening. Bibba wasn't happy about it either.

The first time Hetch showed up at the door I was sitting at the kitchen table with Bibba helping her fold clothes. He knocked on the screen door. He had on a pair of tan shorts, some sort of old dark red t-shirt with a rooster on it and some sandals. I was thinking he should have dressed up a little more to impress Bibba, but he didn't seem to care about that at all. He was all googly-eyed and it made me giggle. He said his hellos and how are yous but I don't think he was paying attention at all. He looked around the living room as he asked where Catherine was. Bibba stepped over and filled up the whole door and told him she wasn't here at the moment. She said, Why might you be inquiring about another man's wife? I put the towels down and moved closer to the door to hear a little better.

I don't mean any disrespect, ma'am. I was thinking she might want to come down to the shop and pick out a new rocking chair. I just made a few new ones. His voice was low and slow and polite.

Something took hold of me at that moment and I blurted out, You make things?

He chuckled. Hey, Jo, good to see you again and yeah, I make things out of wood. How would you like your very own rocking chair?

She doesn't need one, Bibba said. Jo, get back over there and finish up the folding. There's more to be done.

That night at supper I mentioned Hetch offered to make me a rocking chair. I don't think I should have done that now that I can look back on it. Mama looked at Bibba but talked to me and said that she didn't know that he had come by earlier and that yes, he was a carpenter and a good one from what she had heard. He had good work because more people were coming to Wimbee and wanted beach houses built, so he was always working on a house or two. It'd become hard for him to keep up.

I have only heard good things about him, she said, And I don't know why anyone would think otherwise, especially since he is a grown man now. Mama stared at Bibba.

Sometimes I wish adults would just say what it is they want to say. Mama and Bibba sat there and looked at each other and talked with their eyebrows. I watched and tried to move my eyebrows up and down and squench them up and pull them tight just like they were doing and then Aunt Di busted out laughing. I started laughing too and almost choked on the cornbread. Mama and Bibba couldn't keep up their game and joined in on the fun. We all made faces at each other, and Bibba, in between snorts, told us all our faces were going to get stuck. Even David was smiling. It was the first time in a long time I could remember all of us together and happy and it did something to me. I could feel it. Like things were better.

We woke up the next day to find a new rocking chair on the front porch with a big red bow on it. Mama sat in that chair most of the day. I think I caught her crying once but she smiled it away when she noticed me and swore there was nothing wrong.

Later, Bibba took her a cup of peppermint tea and they stayed out there a while. Bibba got up eventually and Mama got up and hugged her. I watched from inside the screen door. Clouds were forming over the ocean. I saw a flash of light way up high, way up in the heavens. It was what Bibba called "heat lightning."

Bibba said, Just know that Nadine's probably already spread some nonsense down at the shop about all this. Next thing you know people will be asking about the fifty piece dining room set he made you.

I stepped out on to the porch. A light breeze picked up my hair and blew strands in my face. Mama, Hetch made you a dining room set?

No, Jo. Bibba's just exaggerating.

I like Hetch, Mama.

Yeah? I do, too, Jo. I always have.

Feels like a storm, Bibba said.

Bibba

May 17th, 2014

My brother, Cal, home from the Citadel for the holidays, was forbidden mentioning *the thing that had happened*. Instead, he whispered to me through my closed door, his breathy words breaking down into millions of molecules absorbed by the wood separating our faces and hearts.

"One day I will find him, Bibba. And I will kill him." But I didn't want that on Cal's soul. He was proof that there are good ones out in the world.

My mother, her appetite having improved to light sandwiches and sweet tea, came to me with a smile on her face. She was no longer late into the mornings in her robe and slippers. She wore a tartan plaid wool skirt that sat high on her waist and then fit elegantly over her hips and her hair was washed and curled and I could see the small, round, clip-on gold earrings she was wearing. I asked her once why she only wore clip-on earrings and she said that nice girls didn't pierce their ears, plus she couldn't stomach seeing her own blood. She still touched up her lips with her deep red lipstick as if nothing had ever happened.

I wondered if I would ever feel like a woman again.

It had been almost a year since my rape. The last thing Daddy had smashed was a grandfather clock given to him by his mother, a clock my mother hated, so she didn't quite mind. I had turned twenty a few weeks before and Mother looked happier than I could remember. She'd always loved Christmas and was busy arranging cut evergreen branches on the fireplace mantel. The chandelier above the dining table was dressed with bows. There were Poinsettias on the front porch and you could see the Christmas tree in the front window all the way down by the mailbox. I was helping her arrange tapered candles in a brass candle tree. She took both my hands with a soft squeeze this time and was delighted to tell me that Connie still wanted to marry me.

"What a lovely boy, don't you think, Bibba? I mean, after

all, your father and I were worried for your future. We just...we just want you to be happy. And now you will be and everything else can be forgotten. Aren't you pleased?"

"Why wouldn't I be happy, Mother?"

Connie was all I ever wanted and, after all, I'd promised.

You must recognize, Jo, that this is how it is for women. I wish I could say *was*, but I know better. My mother was a kind person, smart, actually. She, like most mothers, did the best she could. Men aren't treated the same and thank God, because we know they couldn't take it. Man would have perished long ago. We shouldn't take it, but we do. Yet some times we don't. When we don't, we face a climb up a mudslide. The only way to not end up where we started, beaten and bruised and covered in filth, is by other women standing behind us, their arms outstretched bracing our backs. I can't say I've always been that woman for others. There were times when I should have spoken up, should have chosen differently. And there were times when I couldn't take it anymore, especially when it came to my own daughters. You've married a good man, Jo. You're raising good sons. But don't you ever qualify yourself by their worth. Your worth is your own.

Anyway, the wedding was simple, which was disappointing to Mother, I know, not because she said it, but because she had always discussed my wedding as if it were her purpose for living, her first-place blue ribbon. Well, Cal was really her purpose, but a wedding was certainly exciting! And my father had the money to do it. The Shields family owned property, part of which, was sold off to a golf course developer. Daddy was smart, though, and requested ownership of a small percentage of the course earnings. Didn't seem like a bad deal back then. Nobody thought this small island would attract much interest. But it sure did. Ha! Yes, Daddy was a businessman. But don't get it wrong--I didn't know any of that until after he was dead. We didn't discuss money and as far as I knew, he was a farmer.

I don't recall much planning. Maybe a few questions from Mother.

"Which do you prefer, darling, the one inch or one-and-a-half inch ribbon?"

"For what, Mother?"

"Well, for the bouquet, silly. To wrap around the stems. See? This one is the one, I think." Mother held up a dusty blue velvet ribbon. "Yes. One-and-a-half is perfect. Just imagine this blue with those scarlet and blush roses? We are allowed a few small luxuries, surely."

Surely.

It took me months after the *thing that had happened* for me to go back to church. I never returned to the choir. In fact, I never really returned at all. Someone had cleaned the carpet. Scrubbed away the mess and left a slightly lighter colored patch on the second row. It was all I could see on Sunday mornings. So, I would sing and sing and sing to myself.

As far as Connie was concerned, how wonderful it was of him to take me, ruined, broken, shamed. Well, that's what everyone thought. I saw it on their faces. Pity for me and reverence for him. And maybe he deserved it. But I couldn't stop wondering why. Why would he still want me? He could walk away. That would be okay, perhaps even better to be left alone. Was it for love? Love? What is it? Someone tell me what that feeling is because I wasn't sure, I wasn't sure if I was feeling anything. I was able to stand it only because Connie didn't look at me the same way everyone else around did. It wasn't pity. It was something else like determination. The set jaw, the piercing eyes. I remember it was like he was nodding his head as if he were saying, "Yes, yes, I will do this."

Sometimes, Jo, I see this same look in your eyes.

9

Jo
1986

That was that. I felt a change after Mama and Bibba made up. Aunt Di said Daddy was locked up for beating up that man at the bar. He must have really hurt him bad. Serving ninety days. Ninety days seemed like such a long time. Mama started doing her hair and putting on make-up again, not that she needed it. I watched her smooth cream on her face. She swirled a round, cotton blush pad on her cheeks to make them rosy. Bibba always said she felt naked without lipstick on, so I asked Mama to show me how to do it. I wanted red, but Mama told me to pick a different color. I heard Aunt Di snort as she passed the bathroom. She said, Only hussies wear red lipstick, Jo. I wasn't sure what a hussy was, but it didn't sound good. I decided on a pink lip gloss.

Hetch came by one morning and asked Mama if she'd like to take a walk on the beach. I wanted to go and take Bogue and at first Mama wouldn't let us go, but Hetch said it would be all right with him and so we went, too. I wanted to run and Bogue was always ready to go with me. We would run down the beach and Mama would yell if we got too far. I had on my bathing suit under my shorts and t-shirt. I got myself so hot that eventually I felt like if I didn't go in the water I might just fry right on the beach. Mama said that I couldn't go in the water all the way yet. Hetch asked if he could take me. Mama didn't answer right away. She looked at me. She looked at Hetch. Her lips pressed together hard.

All right, she said, But not too far. Hetch, not too far, okay?

He said, Trust me, Cat.

My daddy never called her Cat. He always called her Cathy.

He took off his shirt and shoes and went in the water in his shorts. I caught myself staring at his naked chest. I'd seen Daddy with his shirt off before. He was real skinny and white. Hetch was tanned and had a lot of curly hair on his chest. He also had a tattoo on his left shoulder. I could make out part of an anchor and then an eagle sitting on top of a circle. There was a skull inside the circle. Looked creepy. I stared at it. He looked at me and said he got it a while ago, when he was younger. He used to be in the Marines. Mama said she'd explain later.

I stood with the water up to my knees until he came and took my hand. I remembered what Mama had said about feeling her hand in his and I think I know what she meant. His grip was strong and my hand felt small with his fingers the size of rolling pins wrapped around mine. Until a big wave hit and knocked me down. My skin scraped against shells and dirt. I was under and could feel the water tugging and pulling at me in all directions and I could hear the swirling of the water. It was so loud. It was all I could hear and my eyes were open and burning and I could see bubbles floating all around but I couldn't tell which way was up, which way was out. I was scrambling to put my feet down somewhere, to find something solid beneath me, to hold me up and let me take a breath. But my body was rocked again and swirled around so that I couldn't tell which way was up. Finally Hetch scooped me out and set me on my feet and slapped my back a few times. The first thing I heard was Mama yelling and her splashing through the water.

I've got her. I've got her, Hetch said.

He was calm. I was spitting water. I wiped my hair out of my eyes and saw my mother standing in the ocean, her rolled up pants soaked to the pockets and her hands covering her mouth. I'm okay Mama, I told her. She kept asking me if I was okay and I kept telling her I was. She patted me all over, checked to make sure I had all my body parts in the right places and then she held my face. She breathed in a deep breath. Maybe she had that same feeling, of not being able to breathe. Standing there in the water, the waves splashing on us, she seemed to be sucking the air down as fast as she could, like she couldn't get enough. She grabbed me hard and I hugged her back. I cried and the tears mixed with the salt on my face. Another wave came and splashed up on our legs and arms and then she let me go. I saw her hold her nose and fall back in the water. She came back up smiling with her hair slicked back and her t-shirt sticking to her body. Her eyelashes were bunched together in little spikes.

Hetch and I laughed.

She laughed, too, and said, I haven't been in the water in so long. I'd forgotten how all this feels.

Hetch said, Oh Cat, you used to love the beach. How could you forget?

It's easy to forget things like that. Sometimes I forget how much I love the swings on the playground, but every time I get on one, float up high, let go of the chains. I'm flying, the wind blowing my hair out of my face. I remember how much it scares me, how much I love it. I remember feeling free. I get goosebumps all over my skin.

Bogue barked and ran along the beach, his ears flopped on the sides of his head, his tail whipped in the wind. I waved and yelled at him and decided to get out of the water and do some shell hunting. Mama and Hetch sat on the beach to dry off. I watched them talk. Hetch would say something and Mama would laugh. They were serious sometimes, too. She shoveled sand with her hand and let it fall through her fingers as she talked. Hetch nodded.

I was shell hunting, of course, but I made sure to keep an eye on them. I liked Hetch. I liked Hetch a lot and that felt different and different can be scary. What was Mama feeling? Seemed that we both liked him a lot, but maybe she was feeling a different kind of thing.

I sat down right where the water stopped rushing in and dug my toes down until I could feel the cool wet sand. I scraped my fingers in the tiny shell pieces and watched the water fill in the hole I was making. I found some wiggles in the sand. I call them wiggles. They're these little shells with an animal inside and they like to be under the sand, not out in the bright sun. I would dig my fingers in the mud and pull back a layer of sand and broken pieces of shells until I could see them and they would wiggle back and forth until they were back down where they felt safe. Sometimes I would cover them back up myself because it seemed like such hard work for those small little things.

We stayed on the beach until it was dark. Well, not too dark. The moon was out and round and bright. Hetch told me to watch out for baby sea turtles hatching.

The mamas dig a hole near the dunes and lay a bunch of eggs. When the babies are ready, they break through the shells and dig their way out of the hole. Isn't that something?

That seems like a lot of work for newborn babies.

That's not the least of it. Then they turn themselves to face the moon and follow the light to the ocean. The moon lights the way.

Isn't their mama there to help them?

No, honey. The mamas go back in the ocean after they lay the eggs. The babies have to make it on their own and sadly some of them don't make it at all. It's a long journey to the water.

That sounds lonely. I wish they all could make it.

Me too.

I stopped to pick up a stick. Hetch and Mama kept walking.

I watched him take Mama's hand. He looked up at the sky.

Maybe it's the full moon.

Mama looked at him. What is?

Maybe it's the full moon that's making me crazy enough to do this. And then he grabbed her around the waist with one arm and kissed her.

I looked away. It didn't feel right to watch. I drew a line with my stick and started to walk again. I let the stick slide across the sand leaving a trail, hoping that when it was time to turn back, it would help me find my way home.

Hetch continued to hang around the house and around Mama over the next few weeks. He'd come over for supper and play board games with me after the dishes were done or we'd all sit around and talk. They'd talk mostly and I would listen. Hetch told me jokes, too. Like this one: What does a frog order at a restaurant? French flies and a diet croak. Or this one: Where did the king keep his armies? Up his sleevies. He was funny.

Mama and I went to his shop. It was a big room that used to be an auto repair shop, he told us. He had big fans facing out of two windows and he showed us how, when he turned them on, they would suck up all the sawdust and blow it outside. There were chairs and tables waiting for stain, piles of lumber, bookcases, cabinets, a fireplace mantel. He showed me all of his tools and let me use a few that weren't too dangerous. I had to wear safety glasses that looked pretty funny. Even with his fans, his work tables were covered in sawdust. I liked the smell. The items on one table caught my eye and I went over to get a better look. I peeked back at Hetch. He told me I could touch them. One was a round wooden box with flowers carved in the top. I traced the flowers with my finger.

Wow, I said.

Hetch smiled.

Mama said, It's beautiful. She walked around looking at each thing he'd made.

Hetch asked me, Would you like for me to make you something small real quick?

Oh, yes please! Can you make a horse? I love horses. I sat with him as his large hands made tiny cuts in a piece of scrap wood. I asked him about his tattoo again.

What does that mean? What's the circle and the skull for?

He looked at me and said, The circle represents crosshairs, what you see inside a scope on a rifle.

I sat back a little. I felt my stomach tighten. Hetch paused his cutting.

There was a time when I had to fight, Jo. You've heard of Vietnam? I was a Marine and it was my job to help protect the men fighting beside me. I wanted to do what I felt like I was supposed to be doing.

He blew on the carving. Thin curls of wood fell to the floor. I watched his thick hands move slowly and carefully. Mama came over and joined us.

He continued talking, I was young. Too young. All us boys were. I was running away from things. I was proud to be part

65

of something big, something noble. That's how it was sold anyway. Now, I'm not so sure what I was looking for a way out, I guess, or a way to forget. When you're older, you might look back on things, Jo, and wonder why you did certain things, said certain things. Life can be perplexing in that way. You look back at yourself, you remember the dreams you used to have, and feel like you're looking at someone you forgot you used to be." He looked up at Mama and then at me. Do you understand what I'm saying?

I told him I didn't know, but the truth is I did. There were times I thought back on living in our house in Lenoir. It's like I couldn't see myself there anymore hiding behind the couch or under my covers or running down the street to get away from all the yelling in the house. Was that me? I didn't want to be her. She was always scared and lonely. Was Mama the same girl I saw in Bibba's picture album, the one who looked confident and carefree? It was hard to see that girl in her now. Instead of telling him that, because it didn't seem like the right thing to share, I told him I really love horses and I hope to get to ride one someday. He carved the horse's mane and everything. It was real pretty, and I decided right away that it would go on my nightstand so that I could look at it every night before going to bed. I asked him to make David a dog. He said he would. And you know what? He did.

Bibba wasn't too nice to Hetch but she didn't tell him to get off her property anymore. It wouldn't have stopped him anyway. Maybe she knew that, too. I can't imagine Bibba ever giving up on something so I decided to think that she and Mama had just come to some kind of understanding. He never stayed after supper for too long, and he always brought Bibba some fresh flowers or some strawberries or peaches. Mama always told me don't be an empty-handed guest. Hetch's Mama must have taught him the same thing. Aunt Di was nice enough to him, but gave him a hard time about his farmer's tan. He didn't care. He kept on coming back to visit.

Until he stopped.

It was the middle of August and normally Hetch walked with Mama in the mornings or came over for a meal once a week, but then he just... didn't. Mama sat in her rocking chair on the porch most of that week, waiting for him. He never showed. I got upset. I was getting mad and sad and upset all at once. I didn't understand what was going on and nobody talked about it, at least not to me. And, that made me mad. How could he be here and then not be here and no one say one thing about it? It made no sense. Finally, I got up the courage to confront Mama about it.

What happened? Why is Hetch not coming to see us anymore? My throat was getting tight and my eyes filled up.

He just can't come over anymore. It's not a good idea.

That's not fair! I couldn't help yelling. I was angry with her but I didn't know why. I guess I felt like it was her fault and she wouldn't explain it to me, which made me feel like a little girl and I wasn't little anymore. I could handle things. Everything was going so well, for once. Why did she have to mess it up? Why was she treating me this way? Why was it that every time I wanted to show Mama my courage I ended up crying and getting upset? It was so frustrating.

I love him, Jo. But I *can't* love him because I'm married to your father. Your Daddy has done a lot of bad things, but it's not all his fault. He's not bad all the time. So just quit it! Go on back inside, will you? She turned away from me.

I was crying then and swung the screen door shut, ran to my room and slammed my bedroom door. Then, I took my wooden horse and threw it against the wall breaking off a leg. I cried even harder, not knowing why I broke my horse like that. I got in my bed and cried for a while, a long time. I don't even know how long. Your father, she'd said. Maybe she would be a whole lot happier if she'd never met my father, never had me. It was getting dark by the time Bibba knocked on my door for me to come eat supper.

10

Come on, Jo. Bibba sweet-talked me through my bedroom door. I refused to come out for a whole day except to go to the bathroom or to take a plate of supper Bibba left for me. I finally opened my door and she leaned against the jamb with her arms crossed. I crossed mine, too. She came in and sat on my bed and patted a spot next to her. I didn't move. She patted it again and so I decided to go and sit down.

Now, she said, Listen here to me. I think you have every right to be mad. I looked up at her and she put her finger to her pink lips to quiet me so she could continue. Your mother is struggling a little bit. And I don't expect you to understand or accept what she is feeling, but either way she is good and wants to do the right thing. Sometimes grownups don't have all the answers. Sometimes we make mistakes. Sometimes we have to ask for help. So, Jo, I am asking for your help.

You need *my* help?

Yes. I need for you to try to forgive your Mama and to be nice to her and tell her everything is going to be all right, because it will, Jo, I'm telling you it will. And that's a promise. She stood up. Now, do you think you can do that for me?

Yes.

Yes what?

Yes Ma'am, I said.

I made up with Mama. She held me close and kissed the top of my head.

Jo, I'm so sorry for yelling, for sending Hetch away, for everything. This isn't what I'd imagined for us. I'm trying to do the right thing and sometimes I don't know what that means. I make mistakes.

Was marrying Daddy a mistake?

Never. Because then I wouldn't have you and David. It was the best decision I ever made.

But, Mama. I don't like it when he hurts you. He's so scary sometimes...I...

Oh, honey. I didn't ever want that. I swear I didn't.

We sat for a while hugging each other. I felt a little better. She told me it was all going to be okay. She pulled David onto her lap. She stroked my hair and kissed the back of David's hand.

But it wasn't okay. I didn't know it then, but Daddy was out of jail and coming for us.

Bibba

August 7, 2014

Your grandfather and I were living in Charleston. It's an incredible city, Jo. So much good food and beautiful houses with beautiful gardens and history and horse shit. And damn hot.

Connie was a working at the hospital there. We were having a good time. He was busy at the hospital. Most of my time was spent on my own, which I didn't mind. I wanted to make a home for us. I sewed curtains and bedspreads and napkins and placemats. I read cookbooks and learned how to make shrimp and grits the right way. I read Agatha Christie, G.K. Chesterton, Dannay and Lee. I prided myself on figuring out the mystery before reaching the end! I walked through the markets and watched men show each other how they do things better than the other, whether it was whittling or butchering meat or whistling a fancy tune; and the women circled around holding parcels and talking about church events. I sat down by the water and marveled at those who were brave enough to drive over The Old Grace Bridge. There used to be just one bridge, you know, over to Mount Pleasant, with room for only one lane of traffic at a time. It was either coming or going. You could get half way over, peering down into the water and find yourself nose to nose with another car. People running into each other. That's why they built the second one, to make a pair, The Old Bridge and The New Bridge. Now they've got the new fancy one, but you won't find me going over it. No way.

Moving to Charleston was good for me. I wanted to embrace this part of my life and not let my mind go back to before. Different people, different streets and shops. It was all so new, which kept me from dwelling on the past. I decorated for Christmas and felt joy again.

A lot of kids moved to Charleston to go to school or work, so it wasn't uncommon to run into people we knew. Nadine was a girl from home. You remember her? Nice enough, I suppose, on the outside. Unfortunately, she has always been immature and gossipy. Connie and I were returning from the market where we visited a butcher who would sell us thinner cuts for good prices. I heard her call my name from somewhere behind me. I longed to disappear, but I didn't want to be rude. Nadine flashed her recently acquired ring in our faces and squealed about her fiance. I can't remember his name. She insisted that Connie and I attend the engagement party her aunt was hosting. That was the last kind of thing I wanted to do, but Mother would have died had we turned down the invitation. Plus, it didn't last. Their marriage, I mean. A few years maybe and then she was back in Wimbee living with her parents.

Her aunt and uncle lived in one of the carriage houses on the Cooper River side of The Battery. Money money. We were living modestly in a one bedroom apartment on the northern part of town. I didn't own a proper evening dress at the time. I did my best with a blue tea-length dress with lace sleeves and a string of pearls Connie gave me as a wedding gift. Connie wore his best suit, his only suit, and we laughed at how the valet was dressed more expensively than we were. It was a crowded affair, which made me uneasy. I was always trying to stay near the door and Connie had to pull me farther in promising not to leave me. I followed Connie past the wait staff who carried champagne and bourbon punch, smoked salmon, melon balls and salted almonds, past the family paintings, almost tripped over a cocker spaniel wearing a bow tie who was scurrying around looking for dropped hors d'oeuvres. We made our way through a group smoking cigars in the library and found the French doors to the courtyard. We went outside and I could feel an immediate clarity, the fogginess that clouded my brain inside the house where it was loud and the air was hazy and the smells were ripe and rich, was lifted and I could breathe again. The light was dim even though the moon was large and full and the breeze moved through the ferns that flanked the French doors and stirred the ivy leaves, their vines growing along the brick wall that surrounded the private garden.

"Woo. There we are." Connie offered me a seat on a bench.

"Yes. Thank you. I much prefer it out here."

"Do you want some punch? I can go brave the crowd and get us some."

I did not appreciate the stillness of the garden until another group of couples found their way outside and it was gone. They were laughing and talking and didn't see us right away. The music inside picked up and voices cheered.

"I'm fine right now. Let's just stay here and cool off for a minute."

Connie turned toward the approaching group and smiled, ready to make introductions, but he didn't need to because one of them was Nadine.

"Oh! Bibba, dear! And Connie! I haven't seen you all evening. What a lovely little string of pearls you're wearing. Are you enjoying the party? Isn't it divine? Have you tried the salmon?"

"Thank you. Everything is lovely, Nadine."

"Won't you meet my other friends?"

Connie and I stepped forward into the light.

"This is my dear cousin, Henry, and his wife, Sarah. You may remember him, he would visit during the summers?"

Two of the gentlemen and their wives turned toward us. The smiling ladies were lovely in their dresses and greeted me politely. I extended my hand to one and then the next. The second woman was Sarah. She had a sunny smile and her blonde hair was swept up framing her face beautifully. Something buzzed at the back of my brain. I'd only half-recognized what it was before her husband Henry stepped forward. A moment before, his face was difficult to make out because of a shadow from one of the porch's columns shaded his face. Connie's arm around my waist tightened. Henry wasn't as tall as Connie, and perhaps, slightly thicker through the shoulders and middle, but it wasn't his appearance that got my attention. It was his voice.

"Perhaps we have met before." Henry said.

Don't make a sound.

I can tell you want it.

My hand flew to my throat. It was closing. I was dying. The world fell away. I searched for my sheet music. There, under my choir chair. I felt like his hands were on me again. Dust and red carpet fibers filled my lungs. My legs gave way, my hands hitting the brick walkway. My shoe came loose and I stared at it. Henry's wife Sarah bent down to me. She placed her hand on my arm and I drew back, not wanting to feel anything.

Nadine made an *oh* sound and Connie said something and they all backed away. He helped me up and sat me on a bench.

"Put your head down, Bibba. Breathe." Connie pushed the back of my head. I couldn't breathe. Don't, don't touch me, not now. I slapped his hand away.

I heard the rapid tapping of heels on the bricks. The women saying something about getting me some water. Nothing made sense and yet it did.

"Get out." Connie's voice was a low muttering. I hardly heard it. It sounded so far away and then I heard that laugh. That laugh from the sanctuary. I looked up. Henry was smiling and his friend looked confused. I couldn't breathe. I saw Connie's fists and I grabbed one of them, but I wasn't strong enough. He launched himself at that man, THE man. Connie punched the right side of his face. Henry's head snapped sideways. Then his friend was there pulling the two of them apart.

"Watch it there, friend. Wouldn't want to cause a scene." Henry laughed again and pulled out his handkerchief to wipe his mouth. The other man pulled him inside.

Connie knelt beside me.

"Did you see it?" I was gasping for air.

"I know, Bibba. I know. I'm so sorry."

"Did you see it?"

"Look at me, please, Bibba. No, no, I didn't see it. I didn't actually see it. I came in to the sanctuary at the end of it all. I was looking for you."

"What?" His words were so confusing.

"I just came in at the end. I didn't know what to do, God, Bibba! I'm so sorry. Please forgive me! I just didn't know. You were lying there. It was so obvious what he'd done. I was so scared you were dead."

"What?"

"Please, Bibba...It's been killing me! I couldn't understand why the Perry twins, my God, the pastor's sons, were guarding the door to the sanctuary. I had to push my way through them to get inside. The way he looked at me when he passed by going out the door of the church. The way he laughed in my face! I'll never be able to forget it."

"No, no. Did you see the brooch? His wife. His wife is wearing my brooch."

My pearl.

11

Jo
1986

Mama seemed happy again even if she wasn't seeing Hetch anymore. Well, she had her moments. She would go sit in the rocking chair he made her and miss him. She rocked David there, drank her tea there, read magazines. But, I think she sat in that chair to miss Hetch on purpose. Is that what love does to a person? Is love always hard and mean? And she'd sit there for a good while and then get up and put on a smile. I still missed him being around, but tried not to think about it too much. Of course, it was awkward seeing him at the grocery store.

Bibba and I ran up to the store to grab a few things for supper. We almost ran over Hetch's foot, he was in front of our buggy so fast.

Don't want to bother y'all, just wanted to be polite and say hello. How is Catherine? His face was scruffy and he kept scratching at it. He had a basket with only a few things in it, some eggs, a couple of cans of tuna, some oyster crackers. Bibba said, She is fine. Don't worry too much about her.

He looked at me and David who was sitting in the buggy trying to eat through the packaging on some cookies. He ruffled David's hair and asked, How is Bogue? I miss spending time with Bogue and playing on the beach. His eyes said he was talking to me.

Oh, he's fine. I'm sure he misses you, too, I said.

Well, make sure that he knows that he hasn't done anything wrong. He's a good dog and if I could have it my way, I would see Bogue every day. I told him that Bogue was just a dog and that I was sure he would be fine.

We got to the checkout line and Nadine, the shell shop lady, was a few lines over. Bibba saw her too and said, Oh the crazy never quits. Nadine saw us and pulled her buggy out of her line. She bumped and pushed her way over, her apologies and giggles leading the way. Bibba breathed deeply and closed her eyes for a minute.

Nadine said, Well hello to both of you! How are y'all today? I see you've been doing some shopping. Me, too. I'm making a strawberry pie while the strawberries still look good. I didn't get my strawberries here, of course. I get those down at the corner. You know that fruit stand? Betsy-what's-her-face just took it over from the Pearsons. You know the Pearsons?

Yes, Bibba finally said. Yes, I do know the Pearsons. How are you, Nadine?

Nadine said, I'm just fine. Then, she leaned close to Bibba and said, I hope Catherine is all right what with Hetch snooping around. He ought to know better than to sniff around a married woman.

Bibba turned on her and said, And what would you know about it, Nadine? What do you know about what someone ought and ought not to be doing? My daughter could be shacked up with the Pope and it wouldn't be any of your business. Don't you have some Goddamn sea shells to hot glue?

Nadine's mouth made a big "o" shape and her eyes were the size of cantaloupes. She finally closed her mouth, turned redder than a cherry and bumped and crashed her way out of line and across the store. Bibba turned back to me and told me to close my mouth. Then, she winked at me. I laughed and started taking our groceries out of the buggy to be scanned. I couldn't believe it. I still think that might have been one of the best moments in my life.

12

It was the end of August and I was real nervous. The third grade had been sneaking up on me all summer. I was trying not to think about it. A new school. New kids. New teachers. New everything. If I thought about it too much, I'd get wrapped up in all these questions. What if no one liked me? What if I couldn't find my class? What if I had to go to the bathroom during class and then I got lost on my way back? What if the kids are all smarter than me, have better book bags and new shoes? Does everybody bring their lunch or do they eat the school lunch? Is it cool to ride the bus?

I had seen some kids around when I was out running errands with Bibba. Once, she stopped at the post office and I decided to stay in the car. I saw some boys walking up the road, laughing and jumping up to hit the leaves on the trees. Why do boys do that? Always jumping trying to reach and smack at things. I sank down in my seat so that I could barely see out the window. I don't know why, but I just wanted to watch them without them knowing. I wanted to see what they were up to. No good, probably. There were three of them. Two of them were scrawny and short and one was big with thick legs. All three of them had sticks. One of the scrawny ones skipped in front of them and turned swinging his stick out like a sword. Stupid, boys. It did make me feel a little better though. Maybe kids are the same no matter where you go. Boys will always be dirty and wanting to play fight and wrestle and not wipe their runny noses. Gross. But what about the girls? Are the girls the same here as they are back home? I hope not. I hope they're better.

My first day at Wimbee Elementary was on a Thursday. I like how they don't make you go back on a Monday. Your first week is just two days. That's pretty good thinking. Quicker to the weekend, anyway, which I like. I was excited. Mama got me some new shirts and a couple of pairs of shorts. I got to choose what I wanted to wear, a pair of light pink shorts with this purple top that had three buttons at the collar going down in a row. There was pink ribbon on the bottom of the shirt and on the sleeves. I had white tennis shoes. And white socks. Bibba stopped me in the hall that morning and told me to go in her room and look under her bed. I found a new light blue book bag with black zippers. It had a big zipper pocket and then a smaller one on the outside. Oh, and black straps. I thanked her and ran to my bedroom to put my notebook, colored pencils, regular pencils and eraser tops in my new bag. Mama helped me adjust the straps. Bibba, Mama and Aunt Di watched while I did a little twirl in the living room. Bibba reminded me to get my raincoat because she said, The summer storms aren't over. It was true, they were hard to predict and the sea winds could push them on land in a flash, when you aren't expecting it. I gave David a pat on the head and told him I'd see him after school.

And then it was time to go.

This new school was a lot smaller than the one I was used to in Lenoir. Mama drove me in Aunt Di's car even though it was only a few blocks from the house and parked where all the other parents were letting their kids out. All the ones that didn't ride the bus, anyway. While we waited our turn, I watched other kids hop out of their cars. I recognized a couple from just around. Kids older and bigger, some not as big. Girls with bows in their hair, boys carrying their book bags with only one shoulder strap. Everybody was eyeing everybody else. Mama looked at me and asked how I was feeling.

Good, I guess. Everything's going to be fine, Mama. Some of the parents were parking and walking in with their kids. I wanted to walk in by myself. I got out of the car and made sure I had my lunch. I straightened my shirt and waved at Mama and then ran back to the car. She rolled down the window.

Can you wait a minute while I go inside? After a while you can go, though.

She nodded. Okay, and then said, Jo, remember who you are. Don't ever forget. You're going to do great.

I found my way to the classroom. I made sure that we left the house early that morning. I didn't want be the last one to find my seat. There were a couple of kids already sitting at desks talking to each other. They didn't seem to notice when I came in. That's okay, though. I saw nametags on all the desks and went around looking for mine. I was in the third row. Pretty good. Kind of in the middle, I thought. I got out my notebook and a pencil. I looked again at the postcard I'd received in the mail. It had my teachers' names on it with the room numbers. This was Room 105 with Mrs. Williams. A girl sat down next me and I looked at her without turning my head. No need to call attention to myself.

Hey! She yell-whispered, scaring me a little. My name is Lisa, see? She held up her name tag. You're new. I'm not new. I like your shirt. She pointed at the two other girls in the room. That's Melissa and Casey. Melissa's dad is unemployed. And Casey's older brother has a drug problem.

What's your name? Oh, yeah. I see it there. Josephine.

I looked down and frowned at the use of my whole name. It's just Jo, really, I said.

She hmmmm'ed. You ever thought about wearing your hair in a ponytail? I got a Scrunchie you can borrow.

Lisa talked a lot, but was pretty nice. She had blonde hair that was short, above her shoulders. Her mama had just cut it, she said. Her eyes were green and she had big ears. She told me one time that she didn't think she'd ever get her ears pierced because her earlobes were way too big for earrings. I told her she could wear clip-ons. She had freckles on her nose and her fingernails were painted fuchsia. The paint was chipped and the skin around her fingers was raw from biting. I saw her do it. She chewed on her fingers all the time. Sometimes they would bleed, she chewed so much. I told her about Mama and me living with Bibba and she said that her daddy wasn't living with them, either. I didn't ask why. We talked for a few minutes before Mrs. Williams started class. We all had to tell our names and something interesting about ourselves to the class. Most of it was kids saying they took dance lessons or played soccer. I said I had moved to Wimbee over the summer. Lisa said she has read the Bible all the way through twice and could pronounce all the hard names. I'm not sure that was true.

Before I knew it, the first day was done. I was exhausted, but satisfied. Everything was okay, just like I told Mama. I wanted to get back to Bibba's so I could tell everyone all about it. By the next week, I had figured out how to get around school. The lunchroom was loud and smelled like weird cheese. On Fridays the lunch ladies served rectangular slices of pizza and green beans with small round potatoes, baby potatoes. They were nice and salty. Lisa sat with me at lunch only she wasn't eating. Most of the time, Mama packed my lunch: a sandwich, some chips, an apple or grapes. I started asking Mama to pack two sandwiches in my bag. I'd give one to Lisa. Sometimes she would eat half of hers and then put the other half in her pocket. She said she just wasn't hungry, but I'm pretty sure she was just saving it for later. Lisa's mother was a hair dresser. She doesn't own the salon, just works there. Lisa said that some days her mama would come home and her ankles would be swole up to the size of watermelons because she has to stand so much during the day. Lisa goes to the salon (it's called Hair and There) after school and sweeps up all the cut hair that falls on the floor.

Most of school was okay. I could read and write in cursive. Lisa sometimes had trouble with long words (another reason I didn't believe her story about the Bible), so I helped her with those. And I was terrible at my times tables, but she was quick with numbers. She said it was on account of having to add up the tips her mother made everyday. She and her mama would put all of it except a few dollars into a secret jar at home. They were saving up to go to Paris, Lisa said. Every Thursday we had P.E. class. That stands for Physical Education. I hate P.E. Ms. F was our PE teacher. No one knew her real name, but some of the kids laughed and said it stood for Fat. I didn't like how she sat in a chair and told us to run laps. I got a cramp in my side and she told me to stick my thumb in my mouth and blow. Or hold my arms up in the air, but to keep running. What good was that? When we were done running, she would tell us to stand on one foot and close our eyes. Whoever could stay that way the longest won. But there were never any prizes. Every now and then, we got to jump rope. That was fun.

And there was recess. Lisa and I liked the monkey bars the best. I liked swinging from one bar to the next all the way from one side to the other. Lisa liked to flip upside down and hang her legs over the bars. I never tried doing that. When we got tired of the monkey bars, we'd race around the playground. I was faster than she was, but she didn't seem to care. She was better at Miss Mary Mack. She could clap her h a n d s s o f a s t . MissMaryMACKMACKMACKalldressedinBLACKBLACKB LACK

I couldn't keep up. Every time I messed up she would start laughing so hard and say, No! Jo! But not in an ugly, teasing way. She didn't make me feel bad about messing up. We sat on the bleachers one day and she braided my hair and stuck a dandelion in it. You've got pretty hair, Jo, she said. Later, I asked Bibba if I could save the dandelion like she had saved the other flowers in the frames on my wall. I liked Lisa.

She told me one day that she gave a note to this boy Steven during homeroom.

Why? I asked.

What do you mean *why*? Because I'm in love with him. She was very matter-of-fact.

In *love* with him? What in the world for?

Well, we all have to fall in love with someone, Jo. Why not him?

Do we really have to? I hoped not.

I don't know why she picked him. He wasn't all that cute, just regular looking like the rest of us. He sometimes picked his nose in class. I figured if you're going to take the chance, choose somebody super special. Otherwise, what's the point? She seemed real happy about it, so I thought she must know he liked her back. But she said she didn't. She said he had taken the note and just stuffed it in his pocket and walked away. I couldn't believe it. I told her I could never do a thing like that. She said, Of course you can Jo, you can do anything you want. That day at recess, Steven and his friend Russ walked up to us while we were on the swings. Lisa stopped swinging. Steven threw the note on the ground and stepped on it. He said in front of everyone, I don't like you at all, and I will never like you! My Mama says your daddy run off because your Mama don't know how to take care of a man. He was sneering. The playground was still. Everyone was watching.

Well, I was mid-swing when I jumped out of my seat and landed a few feet from him.

He said, What are you looking at, ugly?

That's when I slapped him. Russ yelled something at me and shoved me in the shoulders. I shoved him back. I slapped his silly face, too. I heard Mrs. Williams calling from across the playground. She ran over and pulled me by the arm. Lisa tried to follow telling Mrs. Williams, Jo didn't start it! Jo! I'm sorry, Jo! Mrs. Williams snapped at her to stay put. She never let go of my arm all the way to the principal's office. She said, Jo, that is no way for a lady to act.

I turned to look at her and said, I'm not a lady.

Jo, I swear, girl. Mama couldn't even make sentences when she picked me up from school. We sat in the car staring forward. I could see out of the corner of my eye. She was breathing deeply, her nostrils flaring. Both of her hands were on the steering wheel, holding on like she was speeding down the highway, but we weren't even moving. Was she waiting for me to talk? Or was I supposed to wait and listen while she yelled at me? She was surely disappointed in me, thought she could depend on me, count on me. What would she say? I didn't know what to say either. Every time I opened my mouth, it felt like the words just weren't the right ones to say. Why had I done it? I felt so mad when I was hitting Russ. I was just so mad. I was crying, then, in the car with Mama. What did I expect her to say or do? She was upset. I could tell and I had made her feel that way. I tried to tell her how sorry I was, but I was sobbing and coughing.

She reached for me and said, Jo, things have been real hard. I'm so sorry, baby.

And we cried together.
That was a Tuesday.

On Wednesday afternoon the principal came to our classroom. We were going over our vocabulary list. I was watching the rain make streaks on the window. As soon as I saw him enter the room, I felt sick. It felt like a mouse was crawling around in my stomach, scratching at my insides, eating a hole through my skin. I just knew he was there for me. The fight. Maybe Steven's parents were so mad they had called the cops. Maybe I was going to jail. The whole room stopped and we all waited for him to speak. He asked the teacher if he could borrow me for a moment. There was a boom of thunder and a flash of lightning. I knew it. I looked at Lisa and she had this look on her face, like she'd seen a horrible monster come in the room. Everyone was whispering and staring and giggling and Mrs. Williams was shushing. I felt my skin stick to the seat as I swung my legs around to get out of my desk chair. Got my bag, hooked my hair behind my ears and followed him out the door.

He closed the classroom door quietly. I heard Mrs. Williams ask the class to quiet down. There was a lady from the office with him, his secretary or something. He guided me down the hall a few steps. There's been an incident at your house, dear. It's your daddy, Jo. I immediately stopped and turned to him. I felt the principal's heavy brown hand on my shoulder.

What? What had he just said? No. No, he doesn't know where we are. I said.

He said, Yes, your mama just called to warn us. We're to keep you safe here. Miss Gandy is going to take you to my office and she'll get you a nice grape soda.

No!, I screamed. I shook his hand free. I dropped my bag and I ran. I ran down the hall, left those grownups yelling my name and ran out the door. I jumped down three stairs to the sidewalk, swinging around the railing as I went. I ran with the rain in my face down the street, behind the school. I passed the teacher's parking lot and the dumpsters and the basketball courts. There was a short chain-link fence at the back, but I didn't stop. I stuck the toe of shoe in the fence and pushed myself over into a puddle soaking my shoes. I ran down the muddy streets, dodging the low-hanging limbs of the trees. I kept looking over my shoulder expecting Daddy to be chasing me. I had to get home. He'll kill her. He'll kill them all. Please don't be dead, Mama.

I ran and ran and wished I was better at running. I ran passed Hetch's truck stopped at a stop sign. Should I call for him? I was too afraid to stop. I heard sounds coming out of my own mouth but it was like there was something else there with me. Were those my sounds? Crying, maybe, whining. They couldn't be sounds coming from me. I can't feel myself making them. I can't feel anything except a tightness in my chest and the squish of water in my shoes. And then there was the driveway and the mailbox with my grandfather's sign above it: Doc's Dock, and a truck, Daddy's truck. Oh God. Oh God. Oh please please, Mama. Don't be dead, Mama. And I had run all that way, and now I couldn't move another step. I stared at the truck. I gasped for air, leaned against the mailbox my whole body trembling. Water ran into my mouth and made me cough. I sat down, right there in the dirt road at the end of the driveway. I couldn't do it. I couldn't go up there and see him kill her. She's dead. She's probably already dead, and I can't help.

I heard a truck pull up, the gravel shooting out from under the tires. Jo! Jo! I heard him screaming and felt him shaking my shoulders.

All I could say was, She's dead, she's dead.

And that's when Hetch ran up to the house, slipping on the wet rocky driveway as he ran. And I just stayed there until the cops came and put me in the back of one of their cars.

13

September 10, 1986
Wimbee Island Police Station

"Jo?" The detective leaned forward. "Jo, honey. It's okay. I know that stuff is hard to remember." The detective pulled the tape recorder closer and said, "Detective Miller, September 10, 1986. At 9:43 PM. Interviewee, child, age: eight, name: Josephine Evans, daughter of suspect Ryland Evans. I am pausing this interview for a break." He pushed a button on the tape recorder.

Jo ran a hand under her nose. She didn't realize she was crying until she felt a drop fall on her hand. "Is there any food around here? I haven't eaten today."

"Sure, honey. I'll be right back." Detective Miller nodded to the woman who sat in the corner, not saying a word. Just sat there. Miller got up and scooted his chair out of the way. The back of his suit jacket was wrinkled. They were in a small room. One table, couple of chairs. Jo looked around. The woman smiled at Jo. It'd be nice if they put a picture on the wall or something, she thought. Maybe something with flowers in it. Seems like it would help people feel better. She pulled at a strand of her hair. It was still damp. She looked down at the sweat pants and t-shirt they had given her at the hospital. She also had dry socks. Would she have to give them back? She felt the bandages gaping open when she flexed her feet a certain way. The cuts weren't deep. The pain wasn't so bad if she didn't walk. A nurse had patted Jo's head and said, you'll soon be just fine.

Jo heard the clinking of keys at the door. It took Miller a few seconds to get it open. He was a black man, nice, with a mustache and a bald head. He wore glasses to read and Jo wondered how old he was. He was balancing a sandwich, bag of chips, and a Coke in one hand while holding a file of papers in the other. The woman got up and helped him with the door. Jo scratched at the bandage on her neck.

"Here now. Hope you like turkey."

"Oh, yes sir. Thank you." Jo took the sandwich and soda he held out to her. She popped the can and took a sip.

"Okay." Miller pulled his chair over to face Jo. He slid the bag of chips over to her. She picked at the plastic wrap on the sandwich, trying to find the beginning.

Miller readied his tape recorder noted the time as 10:05 PM. The file wasn't all that thick. Miller opened it, shuffled some papers around. "So, you were telling me about your experiences at your grandmother's house. You were saying that you like the beach and you really loved being at your grandmother's. Sounds nice. I always liked going to my grandmother's house, too. Can you tell me anything about the afternoon your Daddy showed up? What do you remember? Anything?"

Jo looked down at her sandwich. She remembered everything. Every last thing. She remembered the mailbox, the end of the driveway. She could still feel how the warmth spread through her shorts. She was standing in a puddle of her own pee mixed with rain and mud. She remembered trembling, shaking. She could still hear the shouts, the screams, the sirens. Even though she was sitting with the detective in this room with no pictures, she felt herself sink to that ground. Heard thunder pound and pound. Rocks dug into her knees. She wanted to push her knees harder and harder into those rocks, stick her hands into their sharp, slick edges, to pick up a handful of them, mud, shells, and rock, all of it, and stuff it into her mouth.

"Jo?"

"Not really anything." Jo said and took a bite of her sandwich.

"Okay. What about once the officers showed up? It says here in these papers that an officer put you in a patrol car? Do you remember that?"

"Yes."

"Then what happened? Did you see your Daddy come out of the house? With your Mama?"

"Yes." Jo sipped her Coke. "He." She pressed the balled up plastic wrap with her index finger and then released it, watched the plastic change form. "He was holding her by the arm."

"Your Mama?"

"Yeah. And David. Cause she was holding him. And he was crying and kicking. And Bibba and Aunt Di were on the porch yelling and crying at Daddy to let her go."

"Did he have anything in his hands?"

"Yes sir."

"And what was it?"

"A gun. He was pointing it at Mama's head."

"Okay. And then what did you do?"

"Well, I got out of the car."

"Did the officer leave the back door open?"

"Yeah."

"Why do you think you did that, honey? Get out of the car,

I mean."

"Because I wanted to be with Mama." Jo's mouth screwed up.

She was trying her best not to cry.

"It's okay, sweetheart. You want me to open these chips?" Miller glanced at the woman in the corner.

"I can do it." Jo opened the chips and wiped her face with the shoulder of her shirt.

"Where was..." Miller looked down at the papers. "Your mom's friend, Thomas, Tom?"

"Who's Tom?"

Miller looked down again. "A Mr.Thomas Hetchings?"

"Oh. That's Hetch."

"Okay. Hetch, then. Where was he during all of this?" Miller tapped his pen on the paper.

"Well, he was standing by the truck. And he was talking real low. I couldn't hear what he was saying. But I remember he had both hands out in front of him. And there were a couple of officers yelling at Hetch to back up. And at Daddy to let Mama go."

"Is this where you ran to the truck?"

"Yeah. Mama was saying to Bibba that everything was going to be okay. That she wanted to go with him. And she was nodding at the officers and telling them that she wanted to go. That everything really was fine. Bogue was beside Bibba growling and she kept having to calm him down and tell him to stay. And then Bibba saw me running and she started yelling for me to stop. That's when everyone saw me. Mama started begging me to please, please stay away and that she loved me. But...I just didn't want to be away from her. And Daddy was telling her to get in the truck with David and I just felt like I would never see them again. So I ran up and hugged her and that's when he made us all get in. Daddy yelled at the officers to move out of the way, not to follow us, that he had his gun and he was good with it. He spun the truck in a circle and drove fast out of there."

Miller wrote on his paper. "Okay. And then y'all were driving and how was he acting?"

"Upset. He was screaming at Mama and pushing the gun on her head."

"And you and David?"

"We were sitting in the middle and Mama had her arms wrapped around us." Jo's voice cracks.

"She was crying. I could feel her body shaking. David's eyes were wide and he was making these grunting noises. Mama was holding us so tight. It was hard to breathe." Jo looked down.

"You know, Jo, you don't have to worry anymore. Your daddy can't hurt y'all anymore." Miller patted her hand. "Can you tell me what happened on the bridge?"

"Daddy had to stop the truck because there were a couple of cop cars and a fire truck parked on the bridge and we couldn't get by."

"Okay. And then what?"

"He opened his door and dragged me out of the truck. I could hear Mama screaming." Miller nodded and looked down at his paper. He wrote a few notes to give Jo time to continue.

"He pointed the gun at me. He had his arm around me. He was so angry. He was shouting and his spit was running down my face. I remember wanting to wipe it off."

"And what were the cops doing?"

"I don't know. It was hard for me to see. Yelling back at him, I guess." Jo pulled at some loose skin on her thumb.

"And then what happened? Jo, was your daddy threatening to shoot you?"

"Yes."

"Did it seem like he was going to?"

"Yes. I was pretty sure he was going to."

"What happened next?"

"The rain started coming down hard again. I heard a gun go off and I thought he'd shot me. He just let me go. And I fell to the ground." Jo rubbed her hands on her pants. "I noticed the gun on the ground and thought maybe I should pick it up, but as soon as I was thinking that, a cop was pulling me away and I saw other cops running to the side of the bridge. I was saying, 'He shot me, he shot me.' But the cop told me I was okay."

"Uh huh."

"So, that must have been when he jumped." She cleared the thickness in her throat. "Did they really shoot him before he jumped off the bridge?"

Miller looked at Jo. "Yes. Yes they did. But, Jo, listen. He's not coming back this time. You understand?"

Jo takes a deep breath and nods.

"You want to take a break, honey?"

"Okay."

"Is there anything else you want to ask me?" Miller sorted his papers.

"I don't know. I think maybe I'd just like to see my Mama now."

Miller talked into the recorder. When he was done, Jo watched him press the button marked STOP. Then, he closed the file.

Bibba

September 10, 2014

You made it. Do you know that? Do you know I miss the young girl who used to come flying through the screen door with my dog right behind her? But I'm also proud of the grown woman you are now. As I write this, I know you're not perfect (who would want to be?), but you're good. You don't know how good, so just try to remember when you look at your children, your husband: you deserve this, my girl.

14

Jo
2016

Jo checks her phone and hands over her key-card to the garage attendant. The card was already deactivated. They did that upstairs along with collecting your office keys and ID badges. The attendant takes the card without a word. He isn't a pleasant man and had never said anything significant to her, but she knows they had a relationship because his son is a former client. The son was typical. A couple of stupid decisions, a bad attitude, but not a bad kid. She had kept him from going down the pike, like so many did, to a life spent in and out of prison for petty crimes, or maybe more significant ones. Prison can beat a person down so that they lose their sense of humanity.

The trauma, the experience itself of being locked away, the fear of the inside, and also, sometimes, the inclusion, the steady meals, and the routine cause such stress and mental anguish that these sons and daughters cannot help but offend again. Jo was often the only hope a family had. The attendant hands her a jar of homemade pickles, no better way to say goodbye.

It is a strange sensation, pulling out of the space in the below-ground parking deck for the last time. It's as if someone dropped a ball of ice into her stomach: cold, heavy, and melting, leaving her feeling afraid she's made a mistake. Josephine Evans Abbott, Defense Attorney. No longer Jo Abbott, Caldwell County Public Defender in Lenoir, NC. The idea, at first, seemed like a violation of the years she has spent in public service. But the money won. They have three boys, three *hungry* boys (Mama, when's lunch? Mama, can I have a snack? Mama, is there more meatloaf?), a mortgage, school loans (thank God Bibba had helped with those), cell phone and internet bills. She and Will Abbott, her always-love, since-they-were-kids-love, no-one-else-ever-love. She hugged and thanked her fellow PDs. High-fived them, accepted their parting gifts, and told them to keep on fighting. Then she apologized for the thousandth time for leaving them, for giving up, for needing more. They were as she knew they would be, humble, understanding, and forever hopeful. She replays those moments as she drives, her eyes blurry as she rises from underground and into the sunshine of the day.

This last day was planned for months. It was October. School and after-care in session. Will's job as a teacher at the kids' school made the logistics a little easier. Used to be that a teacher could go home shortly after school was done. Now, with tests and homework and papers; conferences, emails, phone calls; Will spent the after-school hours tied to his laptop trying to make sense of it all, at the same time trying to remember why he was ever there in first place. So, Jo made sure her last days at the PDs' office were as unobtrusive to their daily routines as possible. She scheduled her transition to a private firm for a few weeks later. She wants some downtime, some time to breathe, some time to psyche herself up for this career climb (she *was* good enough, smart enough, deserving enough), and she needed some time to bury Bibba.

How do you bury a force? Do you dress it up, put it in a box, and throw it into a hole in the ground? No, Jo decided, you have to burn it to ashes, dust becomes dust again so that none of the force is wasted. It's shaken over the ground, the sea; it peppers the air and mixes in our blood. Of course, Bibba was in Jo's blood already. And Mama's. Mama. Catherine. Cathy. Cat. Dumb Bitch. Stupid Whore. Ungrateful, Disobedient, Filthy, Worthless Woman. How quickly Jo's mind turns toward the dark. Those vile hate-filled words slash her stomach, tighten her muscles, and make her wish she, for once, could forget the sound of her daddy's voice. She digs her fingernails into her palm until her father's presence eases back into its corner. Thirty years seemed long enough to know that a man is dead and gone, but Jo is still afraid.

Mama and Mama's sister, Diana, agreed to the cremation. Bibba always said funerals were for the living. Jo thought she was probably right, but still couldn't go without some sort of ceremony. She told Mama and Aunt Di they were going to spread the ashes at the beach, down at Wimbee, where Bibba had found some happiness (she and her husband, who died an early death, his insides corrupted by the ugly cells of cancer) and raised their daughters and kept her name out of the papers, for the most part (there was that time she ran a neighbor off the road, but that's not for now). Bibba never wanted much attention. She wasn't one of those Southern Ladies from the movies, all lace-gloved, always mid-hydrangea-arranging, at the ready bible-quoting. Bibba never went to church that Jo knew; she said her mind was her church and most people didn't understand that and would think she was God-less, to which, she would say, she agreed with them: She was less than God and they would do good to remember that so are they. Always quick with a retort, but

Bibba wasn't rude or nasty or mean-spirited. She wasn't a redneck, either, which is the only other thing Southerners are allowed to be. She did draw out her vowels. She was the *GRAND- mah-thah.* She had a way of turning Jo's full name into something unrecognizable, *Jo-se-FEE-yen.* And even though she did not hold God above Jo's head using His name to force her to be a certain way or to act a certain way or to frighten her (because, didn't they all know that there was enough to be frightened of), she did remind Jo that people have a choice. They can see God or they can turn their backs; either way, no one can hide from Him.

Jo pulls into the driveway. 1940's ranch, double carport, red brick, black shutters, white trim. Small front yard, but the back is big enough for a swing-set and is lined with a chain-link fence. It is home and she loves it. After she and Will were married, they saved for four years to have a down-payment. By then they had one of their three sons and the second on the way. She could see herself, fat-pregnant with Thomas, packing boxes, shooing a two-year old Brian away from the plastic, afraid he'd put the bubble-wrap in his mouth or cover his face or somehow end up suffocating to death at the bottom of a box. Maybe no one would see him hiding in there and close it up, taping over any chance of escape. The Now Jo chuckles thinking about her early fears as a mother comparing them to the realities of having three boys and said to the then Fat-Pregnant Jo, "Get a grip, girl."

She checks her face in the rearview mirror. Is it possible for the color of eyes to change over the years? She swears her eyes used to be more hazel. They're brown in the mirror. Definitely tired. Of course, the idea that you'll ever sleep after having kids was a myth. So many lies about parenthood. There was so much she and Will had taken for granted thinking that if they just provided a safe home, food on the table, and loved without stopping, then life, marriage, kids would all be a straight path. And the gray hair. Lord, have mercy! Where did all of this come from? She puts her sunglasses on and pushes them up to sit on her head, holding her hair away from her face. She runs her fingers through the ends of her mostly dark shoulder-length hair, wondering if she should cut it short, a more sophisticated cut. Maybe to the chin.

A door slams.

She jumps at the loud noise. Her third, her most vibrant of sons, Matthew, runs to her door and she pretends not to notice the four-year old tapping on her window.

"Helloooo, Mommyyyy." He sings.

"Ah! You scared me!" She yells and it pleases her little boy.

She grabs her things, takes his hand, and lets him pull her up the steps into the house. She tells him, as she always does, "I can't wait to hear about your day. I've missed you."

Her guys, all four of them, cooked a special dinner in honor of her last day at work. Well, as told by Tommy, Brian set the table, but didn't really help with the cooking. Brian rolls his eyes, says something like "what a dummy" and pokes his salad with his fork. Will reaches for more bread and smiles at Jo. It's their secret smile. The one that means, I'm here with you, I get you, I love you. It was a slight lift on the right side of his mouth, then an almost imperceptible reach upward of his eyebrows. She almost cries realizing he hadn't looked at her like that in a while. Maybe she wasn't losing him. Maybe she imagined his lessening affections, his loose grip on her hand like he didn't really want to be holding on. Hope is such a drug. It gushes through her veins, her heart pounding loud enough they all must hear it. Hope boosts her, energizes her, and leaves her wanting more.

Will is still so handsome. How is that fair? His gray started showing three or four years ago and it looks so natural, as if it were always there. Not like hers, the ones that showed up overnight and seemed frizzier than the others. His suited his mature personality and quiet funniness. He was calm and accommodating. Jo knows that some men look at Will and think he is a wimp, a push-over, that his wife calls the shots. She is a lawyer and he's a teacher. But those men are idiots. Will and Jo knew each other as kids. Not well. Not as in *we will be in love one day and get away from here and have a good family of our own, you just wait and see*. Not in that way. They knew each other as children but only by name. They started out at the same school, ran down the same lanes, ate the same store-brand peanut butter on white bread. And then one day, when they were almost teenagers, Will saved her.

She doesn't know why she walked into the lake. What a stupid thing to do. It was December, cold enough to see your breath. She was sitting on the bank ripping up fallen leaves. David, her brother, twisted a stick in the ground to make a hole. David stood up and walked to the water's edge. He flung his stick as far as he could. Maybe five or six feet. Still, a soft wind caught the water and the stick began to drift. David turned to Jo and said, "Go in and get it." She said, "No, find another one to play with, ok? There's plenty." He had stared at her. She knew he wasn't going to let it go. Still, she doesn't know why she went in. Why would she do that? Even after she felt how cold the water was, she kept going. Even after she felt her jeans soaked, weighing her body down, she kept going in farther, farther. Shaking and unable to take another step, her feet slipping on the mushy bottom, she remembers her knees giving and the water running over head, her scalp itching or stinging, maybe, because of the cold. She remembers seeing her father's body in the water. It was blue and his eyes were clouded over.

And then nothing.

She can't be sure if she really remembers The Nothing or whether she imagined it. No sound. No light. No feeling. Was she anywhere? She heard the beeping of machines first. Then she felt the warmth of the hospital blankets, and then the tubes in her nose, and the wires on her chest, and the tape on her arm. And she could see Di sitting next her. Di said, "Hey there, Jo. It's your Aunt Di."

"Why am I here?" Jo asked.

"Because Will saved you. He pulled you from the water and ran to get help. Do you remember the water?"

"Yes."

Jo can't recall Will wrapping his arms around her chest and pulling her back up into the world, but she imagines it. When she married Will, she devoted her soul to him.

She looks around the supper table at her sons and sees varying degrees of Will's features. She notices that Brian, at nine years old, is developing the Abbott chin, dimple and all; Thomas at seven is all arms and legs; and Matthew at four has his father's expressive eyes. They are three versions of Will and she loves him even more. She wonders if he still loves her.

15

Catherine

Catherine pulls her wheeled suitcase into the living room and lays a light jacket on top.

"You look good, but aren't your feet going to get cold?" Di yells at her from the bathroom.

Catherine looks down at her bare feet. "Ha. Very funny."

Di is sitting on the tub with her left leg propped on her right knee. She squints at her toes, armed with clippers.

Catherine stands in the doorway. "Thank God you're wearing pants. You could see all the way to Virginia sitting like that."

"I've been told it's a beautiful view." Di grins.

Catherine can't help but snort at her sister's foul mouth. Di has always had a quick mind. Catherine envies her sister, wishes she were like Di and could say what she really feels, whenever she feels like it. She wants the guts. As children, Di was the sister that ran down the street, skirt flying showing scraped knees from rolling in the grass and climbing trees, passing a gaggle of women out shopping who, with practiced determination maintained their puckered lips as they clucked disapproval at the widow's younger daughter.

Di was daring and funny and spirit-filled. Catherine laughs thinking of her sister as a child.

"What's got you tickled?" Di asks.

"Oh, I was just picturing you. Remember when you used to let the boys peak at you?" She'd hung out with boys in shadowy corners, allowed them a glimpse her early breasts. "Ha! You used to charge them a dollar a piece to get a good look."

"Nipple-looking was two dollars. And they all knew they'd get a good punch if they tried to touch. I had my limits."

"And remember Bibba when she found out? Ooh!"

Di laughs. "Oh, yeah. She dragged me home, swatting my behind the whole way and made me show her how much money I had earned. Seventeen dollars. Boy, did she scream. I tried to calm her down by telling her I had repeat customers."

The sisters wiped their faces, the laughter spilling over in tears. Di was sentenced to walking down the dusty road to the Presbyterian Church and stuffing all that money into the offering box for the poor and hungry and homeless. That was ok to Di. She probably would have given the money to someone who needed it anyway. Probably a kid who wanted an ice cream cone. She would buy shoes for the man who slept under the pier, or a Coke for the mailman on a hot day. Di is always taking care of somebody.

"Ok. Scarf? Or no scarf?" Catherine holds up a cream silk scarf covered in small blue and red flowers. She puts it around her neck and then takes it off.

"No scarf."

"I don't need a little color?" Catherine moves to look in the mirror. "It would also cover up my turkey neck."

"You don't need any *color*. But what *will* you be doing about your *face*?"

Catherine leans into the mirror. "My face? What is it?"

"It's old. And wrinkly. I can't be seen with such a person."

Catherine swishes her scarf in Di's face. "Look who's talking."

"What time is it? How much time we got before Jo pulls up and throws us in the car?"

Catherine looks at her watch. "We've got about twenty minutes before she gets here." She walks to her bedroom, smooths out the scarf in a dresser drawer. She hears the back door open and knows Di has gone for a cigarette. She can see into the kitchen. It was a nice kitchen in a one-story, two-bedroom townhouse they owned together. They'd had a little work done to it; replaced laminate countertops with granite, put in new carpet and changed out a few light fixtures. Catherine was proud of what she had accomplished. At least, looking around, she could see some good she'd done. She knows it was pride that kept her from accepting Bibba's offer to buy her and the kids a place to live. But it was something else, too. She wanted to prove that she could do it. She needed to show herself that she could be a mother, take care of her children, stand on her own for once. The problem was Di wouldn't leave. It turned out to be for the best. Being a single-parent was more than she was ready for. Evening and weekend shifts, sick kids, days where the blackness of the past slept next to her, clung to her, kept her from getting up and combing her hair or brushing her teeth or kissing her children goodbye. Di filled in, helped out when she wasn't working at the County Courthouse. Her job in the Register of Deeds office was a God-send, one of those opportunities come by a friend-of-a-friend. It was about time something went their way.

She looks at the black bag that sat on the kitchen table. Why not just leave Bibba there, she thought. There's still plenty of room for us to eat, fold laundry, have coffee and do crosswords. What's the point of this trip? Why the trouble? Because Bibba wouldn't want the show of a funeral, Di had said. She wouldn't want us driving all the way to Wimbee, either, Catherine had said. What would she want? Sometimes Catherine feels like she didn't know her mother; she didn't know the woman her mother was. She knows she and Di were loved. The worry and nagging and differences of opinion were ways Bibba showed her she loved her. Bibba was always trying to teach them how to make the right choices. But how did she know what was right? When her father had his affair, Catherine wanted to shake him, but he already felt so far away. What if she shook too hard and he left forever? She shook her mother instead. Bibba must have done something to make him do it. If she hadn't been cold to him, if she'd run to him as soon as he came home from work, if she'd just shown that she cared. If, if, if. Of course, Catherine now knows what her mother didn't tell her then: men aren't always what they seem. And sometimes they are exactly what you think they are. It took her a long time to see her father's imperfections. She even knew about the other affairs. She could hear him whispering on the phone, saw him looking at other women. She didn't want to believe it.

Not Daddy who says he loves me, too.

Catherine sits on her bed. Her eyes land, as they often do, on the round wooden box. It sits on her dresser. Whenever she opens it to retrieve a pin for the lapel of a jacket or to stow away a note from a grandchild, she first runs her fingers over the floral carvings touching each carefully cut curve.

But here we are. Packed and ready to go. How many times have I packed my things for a place I hadn't planned on going? Was I ever really going anywhere? I always ended up in the same place. Hetch, are you listening? I'm so sorry, darling. It should have been you, a million times over, it should have been you. You broke my heart once, a simple thing. God, how I adored you. Young and stupid and strong-headed. You tried to do what was right. I shouldn't have punished you for it. That girl punished you enough. I can't imagine having a child in the world and not knowing where he is. What does he look like? What does he do? What are his dreams, his favorite flavor of ice cream? Why couldn't Bibba see that you tried, that you were hurt, that you never meant to hurt me? Why couldn't I see that? I wish I had had more courage.

She can still seem him, a lanky teenager, his arms outstretched, pleading with her, his voice breaking.

"Cat, please!"

"You can't do this to me, Hetch. You left me. I know you did it because you were trying to do right by her. But you did leave. And I felt like I was dying. There was nothing that made me better. You are in my head all the time except now I see you with someone else. In someone else's arms. It's killing me."

"But I'm here now. You can't imagine how hard that was, to have to choose, but it's over. We can be together. Don't do this, Cat. Please don't marry him. Please. I don't care what your mother says about me. He's the one that's not good enough for you. He won't treat you right. I'm the one that loves you. Me, Cat. I'll do whatever it takes."

And she sees him as the man she met again that summer, *the* summer, and on in to a September, that lasted a lifetime. Before, they thought they were grown. Seeing him that summer, she realized how ridiculous it all was, the way they saw themselves when they were but children playing at being adults. The man she saw then was a man who had gone to war and survived. And she, a mother of two children trying to escape her life.

And hadn't she also? Survived?

They stood on the beach. Their arms crossing and uncrossing, hands on hips, hands in the air, eyes streaming and voices rising. The wind caught her hair and whipped it around her head, her words tangled in the strands then loosed to swirl and fly away.

"Please, Cat. Tell me you know he isn't going to change! Tell me you won't go back to that son-of-a-bitch. Promise me."

"He's my husband, Hetch. I'm not making promises to another man."

"Another man? Is that what I am? Just another man?"

"You know that's not what I meant. You know what you mean to me."

"Dammit, Cat. He isn't going to change! Think about Jo and David."

"What do you think I'm doing? Why am I here? Don't you dare do that. Of course I'm thinking about my children. I know he isn't going to change. But that doesn't mean that I can move on with you like he doesn't exist. I'm still married. That matters. What am I showing them? What kind of example am I giving them if I let myself..."

"Love me? Think about me? Want me?" He reached out holding the hair out of her face.

"Don't."

"What if we showed them what real love looks like? That it isn't fear and violence and punishment? That love is respect and kindness and understanding. I know your heart, Cat."

She took his hand away from her face. "If love is respect, then you shouldn't be here. We shouldn't be doing this."

"I wish you could see the life I've dreamed. I've been waiting for far too long for it to come true. I don't think I can do it anymore."

"I never asked you to wait."

"No, you didn't." He stepped away from her. "And you're not asking now."

You were so young, all you boys were, when they sent you off to God knows where. Saw, heard, and did things the human spirit should not have to bear. But then, if I hadn't married Ryland, there would be no Jo and David. And the grandchildren. I wouldn't have them either. That's what got me through, you know. I have a lot of regrets, but they aren't some of them. You would have been a better father, were a better father for a time, but so much damage was already done to my babies and to me. I didn't want you to have that responsibility. I could have given in and stayed with you, but I was so ashamed. I couldn't stop thinking about how different the kids would be if I had been strong enough to spare them the pain.

She usually tries not to spend time with these kinds of thoughts, but her mother's death has made that difficult. Memories come back in a rush sometimes.

She rubs the joints of her left hand. Her fingers never healed properly after her hand was broken some thirty years ago. The hand had been a mistake, Ryland had said. Her husband had squeezed and squeezed until she could hear them popping like twigs. She begged in between gasps of breath, Ryland Ryland Ryland please please. She was on the floor trying not to vomit. He was kneeling beside her, whispering to her. He was sorry, so sorry. But she shouldn't have provoked him like that. Couldn't she see? How many times has he told her? Get up, Catherine. He hated to see her hurt. She was so stupid to make him angry. Come on and get up now. It's over and he's hungry for supper.

Ryland didn't want her to see a doctor. The hand was too visible, too obvious. It needed a good story. Falling down the stairs was a common lie, a signal of a threat at home. At the hospital she told the nurses a more believable story. I slipped on the wet kitchen floor, she said while staring at untied shoes, laces showing dirt like they belonged to some pitiable child. They nodded and looked at her with eyes that said we don't believe you but a man's house is private, which was a joke because everybody in town knew the truth. His daddy, Bull Evans, was the same. A good teacher to his son. His mama, Sally, was all the women in the world who've ever been beaten down, threatened, hauled around by their hair, punched in the stomach. She wouldn't look at Catherine when they'd met (the one time), perhaps afraid she'd acknowledge the Evans Woman's secret. They never visited, preferred to stay on their private property down in Wimbee, far from side glances and groups that parted on account of a violent reputation. Catherine thanked God that Bull and Sally stayed away because nothing was worse than having a man feel the need to show up his father.

Di opens the back door, returning from her inspection of the grass behind their townhouse. Catherine slides her feet into her shoes and adjusts her bedspread. She watches Di swat at the knot on the top of the black bag, not knowing how else to react to their mother's presence on the table.

"Do you think I should have visited David before going today?" Catherine asks coming out of the bedroom.

Di turns to face her. "Honey, he isn't going to know the difference."

Catherine nods. Her son's doctors had him sedated. His outbursts had become too hard to control. He struck the nurses, threw his food, refused to attend his therapy sessions. Catherine's heart was torn in so many directions. She knew it was all because of what he saw as a boy. What she let him see.

He had been a fitful baby. He was never right. She felt guilty for thinking that, but she knew it was true. As David grew out of his babyness, his peculiar and disturbing behavior increased. Banging his head on the floor, pulling lizards apart with his fingers, hardly speaking. He would hide in the dark. She would call and call his name. She panicked not knowing where he was only to find him in the corner of the closet. He did learn to speak and read, but couldn't keep up at school. Catherine finally had to pull him out, trying tutors at home, which she struggled to afford. None of them lasted long. Why hadn't she gotten help sooner? Why was she scared of what doctors would tell her? The child wasn't interested in making friends or playing baseball or going to movies. Before David was even a teenager, he had grown as tall as his mother. Catherine realized she was afraid of him.

Di was right. David was where he needed to be.

Di picks up the black bag.

"That bag is an eyesore." Catherine says.

"You think she cares?" Di points at the bag.

"No, I suppose she doesn't."

Bibba

November 1, 2014

I know all too well how heavy the pall is, cast over your life, smothering and suffocating. And how hard it is to get out from under it.

Today is my 60th wedding anniversary. I try to remember if our wedding was a happy day. I think it was, in some ways. I did love Connie. I just didn't love myself and couldn't see how he would love me either. I felt sorry for him. I was ruined. I felt like a phony bride. I went through the motions and smiled the smiles. My three cousins were my bridesmaids and Cal and two of Connie's school friends stood as groomsmen. Having Cal near me helped to settle my nerves. I remember locking eyes with him once during my walk down the aisle. He gave me a nod, just a quick one, and I knew he was telling me I could do it. I would make it.

Several months before, Mama and I went to a seamstress for a bridal gown. The seamstress showed us several fabrics. I remember touching them, feeling the silky smoothness on my skin and thinking it was for someone else. This beautiful white fabric was being ordered and measured and cut and pinned and sewn for someone else. The design had a full length ball gown skirt with a lace overlay, lace sleeves and a boat-neck collar. Some girls in that day were wearing tea-length dresses, that was the new fashion anyway. That wasn't for me, though. I wanted to be covered. I wanted to hide. When it came time to try it on, it didn't need much altering, which was a blessing because I could hardly take standing there while the seamstress's hands gathered the fabric at my hips, plucked pins from the bust line, and fluffed the skirt around my legs.

Mother picked out blue dresses for my cousins to match the blue ribbon on my bouquet. I have pictures somewhere, Jo. You'll see that it did have the look of a lovely wedding.

And truly it was. I just wasn't myself anymore. I didn't know who I was as I stood there and vowed to love and cherish and obey. The idea of standing in front of a church of people nauseated me, especially in that church. Could he be in the crowd? Was he lurking there, waiting to catch me alone again? At the time of the wedding, I still didn't know what he looked like. He could have been any man. And he was every man with the exception of Connie, my father, and Cal.

It's funny to think how pleased Mother and Daddy were once Connie and I had married, lived in our own home. Settled. When Connie appeared at the church the day we were married, Mother was visibly relieved, but Daddy didn't breathe until our vows were complete. When you're afraid for your child, it changes everything. You do and say and want things that perhaps you wouldn't have in different times. I don't blame my parents. They were good people. You should know that, Jo. There was a certain future they dreamed for me when I was an arm baby. All parents have them. Except, the fear of losing that dream for me became very real. Connie could have run, escaped, married someone else who had the shine still on. But he showed up and wasn't that grand? Wasn't he a dream come true? Chivalry was not dead. But my insides were.

Real disaster was averted.

Thank God we chose the one-and-a-half inch ribbon. Ha!

The day after Nadine's engagement party, it was as if I were right back on the floor of the church. I could not move from bed. I could not make sense of the world. My body was not my own. My husband was a man I didn't know. What I came to realize in addition to the memories that wouldn't stop, caused me to jump unrestrained into a darkness. His name was Henry. He had a name. How dare he have a name, a face. A wife. Does she know? Does she know where that brooch came from? It wasn't until after the party that I

113

realized I had lost the brooch. But of course I had. I was wearing it that day at the picnic and then, later, as Mother helped me into a bath, I stared at my torn and stained clothing, which she lifted with shaking hands, tears running down her cheeks. No brooch. It just wasn't there.

Because he'd taken it.

When Catherine told me she was going to marry Ryland I couldn't help but think of my own mother hand-washing the blood from my skirt, as if I'd ever wear it again. The mind is incredible, don't you think? There I was in the living room being confronted by Catherine and these memories come flooding in. It was mainly my mother's face. How sad and terrified she was. She kept saying, "I'm so sorry, I'm so sorry." I wanted to shake Catherine, to tell her how worried I was, to beg her not to marry him. Because can't you see, Jo? I was losing the dream I had for her. And instead of holding on to her, to the daughter that was standing in front of me, I reached for the dream. I could no longer tell myself that she would lose interest in him, that it was soon to pass, a phase even. I knew she still hadn't forgiven me for running Hetch off. Hetch was not a bad boy. I did know that. But these men. They don't think! They take what they want and leave us with shredded hearts. She needed time to get over him. I wanted more for her and Diana. But all I did was push her away and then send Di to look after her.

I don't know, maybe Hetch would have been good to her. Can you imagine how different things could have been? Connie would have seen that.

Lord, Connie would have told me to stop, to let go, to let her be happy with Hetch.

So, I did a thing. I'm not proud of it. I don't think I would do it again if I had the chance. Did you know that Hetch chose her and that I knew it, had the proof in my hand, but didn't tell her because I thought I was protecting her? Secrets are powerful things. Connie would've known better. He wouldn't have allowed it. But what did he know about truth and lies and protecting people that you love? Connie was dead and any part of me that ever was sympathetic toward love was dead, too.

16

Jo

Jo feels a tug at her shirt hem and takes a break from counting out the cash she has in her wallet. She feigns surprise and says, "Batman! What are you doing in my house?"

Matt pulls off his mask. "It's just me, Mom!"

She hugs him close. "So, Bruce Wayne, you going to keep things in line for me while I'm gone?

"Yep. But I'd much rather keep you here with me." Matt's blue eyes, *Will's* blue eyes, look up at her. She runs her hand over his head. He's grown overnight. She vows to stop feeding him.

"I know, Love. I don't like being away from y'all, either. But, it won't be that long. And while I'm gone, you're going to have fun doing all kinds of boy things with Daddy." Jo picks up the stack of bills, straightens them, and slides them into her wallet. *Always have cash*, she can hear her mother saying.

"Like school. So much fun." Brian has his backpack slung over one shoulder and his hands in his pockets - his new thing, acting like he can't be bothered with school. He's always liked going to school. He excels in everything he does, has friends, but he's started to pull away. He doesn't want to hug her anymore. She's no longer funny, only embarrassing. Where she used to provide comfort, she now irritates. The instant she noticed, she started asking Will questions. What's he like at school? Is he being bullied? Are you not telling me something because you think I can't handle it? Do I need to go in and talk with his teachers? Because you know they told us to put him in this advanced math and remember how I wasn't sure, thought maybe the pressure might be too much? I mean, it's the third grade. It's not like he needs to know all this advanced stuff as a third grader. What's the pace of that class? Is it stressful?

Will had thrown up his hands to block the onslaught. "Hey, hey, hey. There's nothing. It's nothing. He's just...figuring things out."

"What things?"

"Yeah. You know. It's the natural order of things. He's becoming a *guy* instead of a *boy*."

"Is this some kind of code for something? Is this a penis thing? Has he started having erections? Like real ones? I mean, he's nine. Not fifteen."

"Whoa. No. Please. I don't think that's what this is."

Jo's big eyes stare at him.

"What I mean is, yes. Or—no, to the penis thing. Yes, it is about his maturing. He's getting older and he's naturally growing away. It's what happens. They also start caring about how they look, what kind of shoes they have, jeans, whatever. It happens to the girls even faster. You remember what it was like."

She considers what she remembers about being nine and thinks it was nothing like that. Her nine was much different. Thank God. Will knows that, too, and his face contorts.

"Sorry. What I meant to say is that it's normal."

"Well, at least our children are having a normal childhood, right?"

His nine wasn't normal either. The day Jo was sent to the gas station to buy her Aunt Di some smokes, the day the police were questioning her mother at her house in Lenoir, Will was trying to figure out how to tell his dad he needed him to be his dad. Mrs. Abbott, Will's mother had a stroke in her garden the spring before. She was out watering the hydrangeas. It was a wonder she didn't drown. She'd fallen over with the hose running in the grass, face down, water running over her nose and mouth. Some neighbors saw her and ran to help. Will's father was devastated by her condition. Mr. Abbott wasn't aware at how much he depended on her until she was no longer available to be the one who loved. Mrs. Abbott was severely disabled and needed care her husband and son couldn't give her. It was like she'd died. But Will couldn't mourn her because she wasn't actually dead, just changed. Sometimes, as a boy, he wished she had died, felt like it would be kinder. Instead, he visited her and prayed that this week would be the week she would lift her arms and wrap them around his shoulders.

Jo looks at Brian as he shifts his backpack to his other shoulder. She pulls him in close for a hug. He resists slightly, but hugs her back. "I'm going to miss you. I love you." She says and then whispers in his ear, "Whatever is going on, it's all going to be okay."

"Okay, Mom. I know." He rubbed her words off his ear.

Will walks in while tightening his watch band on his left wrist, part of his morning ritual. Tommy is the the last to come in to the kitchen, still in his Super Mario pajamas. Oh, dear. He has always been her sleepy child. Mornings with Tommy consisted of prying him from his bed, dressing what, she imagined, it would be like dressing a floppy mannequin, and hoping he woke up enough on the way to school for him to have something to eat in the car.

At the sight of Tommy, Brian lets his bag slide down his arm on to the floor.

"Oh, great. He's not even dressed. We're going to be late."

Brian hates being late.

Jo makes eye contact with Will and he nods. "I'll be right back with some clothes, okay, Tommy? Go ahead and say goodbye to Mom."

"Where are you going?" Tommy asks. "Oh, yeah. To pour Bibba on the beach."

"Well...okay. Something like that. I love you, Bud." She hugs him. He's still bed warm. Jo looks at her boys and says all the things moms say as she goes out the door. Be good. Listen to Dad. Do your homework. Have a great day at school. At least it's Friday! And, oh, remember who you are.

"And remember to wear your underpants!" yells Tommy, in an uncharacteristic jolt of morning energy and laughter.

"Poop!" Yells Matt because he's four and poop is fascinating.

She hears Brian laugh and say, "Y'all are so dumb."

She listens to her home. It all sounds so normal. Like love. Her throat feels swollen and she swallows hard. How often does she wish she could just read a book or watch a movie, have some peace and quiet, but when confronted with it, she misses the noise, the chaos, the distractions of her every day. When Brian isn't there, she misses his love for music and how he sings when his doing a mindless task like putting away his laundry. If Tommy isn't there, she misses him refusing to close the door while he takes a shower so that he can yell a play-by-play: "I'm soaping my hair, mom! I washing my body now!" And Matty. Whenever he isn't with her, she feels the absence of his body. He has always needed her physically and she has become accustomed to his hand in hers or his head in her lap.

But she needs to leave, she needs to leave now!

Will comes out into the carport telling the boys to get their stuff together, brush their teeth, so on and so forth. He walks around her car inspecting, well, she didn't know what, while she situates her bags in the trunk. He kicks her front tire.

"Car's all gassed up?" he asks.

"Yep. Ready to go."

"Thelma, Louise, and Jo." He hugs her.

"Not likely" She pulls him closer. "I'll call when we get there." He makes a *mhmm* sound. "Hey," she grabs his hand and squeezes. Why does she not want to go? She's scared. She's afraid to leave them. She wants to stay and listen to her family's voices. She's afraid of coming back and finding him gone, the kids gone. The thought makes her drop her keys.

"You okay?" He narrows his eyes, cocks his head to the side. He knows she's upset. She considers taking the jump, diving in, all the way in. Just being upset. Letting it happen. Crying, blubbering about everything, her fears and worries. Ruining his shirt, making all of them late, scaring the boys.

"Oh. It's fine. I'm fine. I just think I'm a little nervous about the trip." She smiles and shakes her head. "You know how I am. It'll be fine."

He looks at her knowing it's more. He nods once and leans in. She gives him a kiss.

"Love you." He says.

"Always." She says and closes her door, wishing she knew how to swim.

Two old biddies by the side of the road. Jo pulls up to the curb in front of the two-bedroom townhome that Mama and Aunt Di share. It was a nice place and Jo was excited when her mother and Di had found it. It was only a twenty-minute drive from Jo and she felt like that wasn't too far and just close enough. Mama had wanted to do things on her own. Maybe she had something to prove. But Di being Di, Mama wasn't doing it *all* on her own. Di was there every step.

Jo looks at her mother and aunt sitting on their luggage by the mailbox. They were like two dogs from the same pound. Mama was an elegant poodle with white freshly curled hair, neat navy slacks, white button up shirt, white cardigan, brown slip on shoes. She sits with her thin legs crossed, hands folded in her lap, elbows tucked in at the sides, trying to take up the least amount of space possible. The other was, Jo imagines, a dog that snarls and bites, a round yippy dog. An underestimated will-cut-you-as-soon-as-look-at-you dog or woman. Aunt Di, God bless her. Here she is in jeans and a sweatshirt and tennis shoes, long gray hair hanging down to her oversized and looming bosom. In one hand she holds her sunglasses, which she is currently waving around making a point about something, and in the other her lit cigarette. Younger than Mama by a scant year, she was also not quite as beautiful in their day, not quite as tall, not quite as thin, or as popular, and on and on. But she and Mama acted like twins, as if they didn't know they hadn't shared a womb. They were a set. Salt and pepper. Not one without the other. Even when Mama married Daddy and made excuses for Daddy and went back to Daddy, Di still saw Mama as her other half. She was one loyal bitch.

Jo rolls down the window.

"Hey, Ladies. Need a ride?" Jo does her best Groucho Marx.

Di stands pulling up her jeans. "Well, well. She finally shows."

"Still all tits and no ass I see, Aunt Di."

"Jo!" Mama stands up holding her small shoulder purse

tightly under her arm. "I can't believe how you talk sometimes. You don't say those things around the boys, do you?"

"Mom, they're the ones that taught me those words."

Di laughs and coughs for far too long. "Pop your trunk, girl."

Jo gets out, lifts the trunk lid, and helps the ladies with their baggage. Di lifts up a black garbage bag, not one of the big ones, but one of the small ones made for office trashcans. There was a rectangular box in the bag, its shape made clear by the box's edges. The bag was tied into a knot at the top.

"Hello, Bibba." Jo says to the bag.

"I don't know why you had to put her box in that rude bag." Mama says as she and Di climb into the backseat. "The box is perfectly fine on its own. May as well just throw her in the dumpster."

"She probably would have preferred that." Di says. "What do you want me to do? I didn't want her spilling all over the floorboards of the car. Here, Jo. Put her up there on the passenger floor." Di passes the bag up front to Jo.

"Are y'all both riding in the back?" Jo looks at the two women in the rearview mirror. They look back at her, incredulous.

"Yes." They answer together.

They were doing fine. About an hour and a half down the road before they had to stop. Mama says she worries about her circulation sitting for too long and Di says good because she needs a smoke and how about food because they ate at five A.M. this morning.

"Want to stop at this Bojangle's-slash-gas station up here?" Jo asks.

"Whatever y'all want is fine with me." Says Mama.

"Fine." Says Di. "I do like a biscuit."

Mama smirks. "And a biscuit likes you."

"Oh, hush. You see all of this?" Di motions to her body. "A shrine for all to gaze upon."

Mama goes inside to find the bathroom. Jo sends Will a text while she watches Di roam around the truckers' lot smoking her cigarette.

at Bojangle's with the broads. Going ok so far. Love you.

She knows he is teaching, but she read somewhere to send your man messages throughout the day, remind him that you LOVE him, that you think he's SEXY, use fruit emojis to describe the kind of salad you will make him or something like that. Wasn't that what kept marriages alive? She wonders if all it will do is annoy him. Who comes up with that stuff, anyway? There was a woman who wrote a book about marriage and said a wife should meet her husband at the door wrapped in only cellophane. Jo giggles. How many ways could that be a disaster? The husband saying "Hi, brought my boss home for..."

Mama is inside the gas station walking up and down the aisles. Get gas, eat food, use the bathroom, buy shades and shot glasses and Christmas ornaments, but don't buy maps because nobody buys maps anymore. Jo goes inside. Mama is looking at the maps.

"Look at all these places. The whole United States. I've never even seen half of them and certainly never will. Can you imagine me in California or Seattle?"

This is Mama's kind of humor, sad humor. She's putting herself down, pointing out her frailties, like her choice to marry Daddy and not go to college. She'd come home from the store and say things like, "You better double-check these oranges I got because you know my picker never was very good." She gave up opportunities for an education, for travel. Her refusal of a better future. If Jo asked her about a headline in the news Mama would say, *Oh, you know I don't know anything about that.* Most people don't pick up on it, but Jo does. There's nothing to be done. No sense in pointing it out. It's certainly not a call for pity. Never pity. And then again, maybe it was just an innocent joke.

"You ready, Mama?"

"Oh, yes. I was born for the road." Mama stops and places her hand on Jo's arm.

"So, tell me. How is Will?"

Shit. She knows. How does she know? How is that possible?

"He's fine. What do you mean?" They continue out the door toward the car. Di is making her way back.

"Well, good. I just was wondering because I thought, you know you're my daughter and mothers can tell. Lord knows Bibba always could. I thought you said something on the phone the other day sounded like you were stressed." She waves her hand in the air like the tension is some kind of smoke she can waft in another direction.

Jo finds this to be a ridiculous thing for her mother to say. There were times, when she was younger, she had wished her mother would ask her what was wrong, but instead her mother sat staring out a window at nothing. Jo wasn't doing well in school, the teacher wanted a conference, but her mother kept forgetting to show up. Di went instead. The first time Jo had her period, she thought she was dying. Bibba was visiting and found her crying on the bathroom floor. She started waking up in the middle of the night to find David crouched in the corner of her room in the dark.

And yet, in Mama's times of clarity, she was exactly who Jo needed. Mama's clarity never lasted long enough.

"You know, I just love Will. He is such a wonderful husband."

"Yes, I am aware at how wonderful my husband is, Mama. Nothing's wrong. We're just a married couple. With kids. And jobs. The normal stuff. Don't worry. I'm not screwing it up." *And what would you know about normal stuff in marriages, anyway? Do you see me, Mama? I need for you to understand that I am good, too.* Jo is annoyed and she knows why. It's hard keeping things from her mother, always has been. So hard to hold on to her resolve. She knows where this is headed: Jo will confess her feelings and end up an emotional mess at her mother's feet. It's happened before. And while she must admit to its cathartic benefits, it also makes her feel like a little girl again, something she tries earnestly not to do. She prefers her adult self. Fortunately, Di shows up at the right moment, just like always.

"Hey, you slow-pokes ready? Got a bag of biscuits." Di smiles.

"Another time." Mama says to Jo as she gets in the car.

Di raises an eyebrow at Jo over the top of the car. Jo rolls her eyes.

How does she do that? How does she know these things? Maybe I just don't want her to be right. It's not her, it's me. I'm annoyed with myself. Not with her, which is even more annoying because it means it's my fault. Why am I not one of those mothers that can tell things about her kids as soon as they walk in the room? Why can't I talk to Brian? Is there more to it than just growing up? And I just can't see it? Why can't I see it? How do I fix it if I can't see it?

"Jo? Jo, did you hear me?" Mama asks from the back.

"Oh, sorry. No. It's this slow driver in front of me. What did you say?"

"Did you want a biscuit? You should eat." A small hand holding a red package appears in between the front seats.

"It's got bacon on it." Says Mama.

"Well, then it must be good." Jo says taking the biscuit.

"You know it. It's why God invented pigs." Di laughs.

"There are certain sections of the population that would disagree with that statement. Cloven hooves and all." Jo says, biscuit in one hand, steadying the wheel with the other.

"All right, Ms. Juris Doctorate." Di spews biscuit crumbs.

"Don't cows and sheep have cloven hooves, too?" asks Mama.

"Sure," says Di, "but pigs don't eat their cud. Considered unclean. Filthy animals." Di winks and then continues, "I knew a Rabbi once. Hell of a guy."

Mama pushes Di's shoulder. "Di, really."

"What? I did. Forgot his name, though. He walked around town a lot.

"Yes, I remember him." Mama interjects. "He had a kind face."

"Had one of those hats, the black ones."

"Now you're stereotyping. What exactly is your point?" Mama asks.

"Nothing. Just knew him, is all. Talked once or twice. Even had one of those numbers printed on his arm."

Mama takes a deep breath, "God bless him."

"No joke. I remember his obituary in the paper. Long, lot's of schooling. Impressive guy."

"Oh, you know who died a couple of days ago?" Mama asks.

"Who?"

"Mrs. Basa."

"Mrs. Basa?"

"Yes. The Filipino woman who lived down by the gas station?"

"Oh, yeah. She used to sell lumpia from a big freezer chest in her garage. That stuff was good. How'd she go?"

"The paper didn't say."

"Probably rolling out a thousand of those pastry wrappers, pinching the ends, and then BOOM. Dead in her kitchen."

"For heaven's sakes, Di. She was a hard worker, though. You're right about that."

Jo isn't surprised the conversation had come to this. It seems like these two are always talking about who died, who was sick, who was having hip surgery, or who got lost walking the dog. Jo imagines Mrs. Basa at her kitchen table, her hands covered in flour and smiles. Everyone would miss her. The Rabbi, too. Jo scratches at her wrist and considers the level of evil it would take to permanently mark someone's body as if he were property. A chair, a rug, a cow, a dog, a boy. How less than he must have felt. How utterly in despair. She doesn't know this man, but she feels for him. She imagines a small boy separated from his family. She sees him in the black and white photos of the Holocaust camps. She sees children, frail, sick, tortured, and barely clothed standing behind fences in the snow. She sees her children's faces and her heart catches in her throat. Then, she sees an image of David, a child in black and white. A grim expression and she knows there is no saving him.

It wasn't nearly so bad for me. Lots of kids had it worse. We were never starving, never out on the street. Daddy came home drunk. Daddy beat Mama. Daddy yelled at me and David, telling us we were nothing, no one, no better than the spit in his cup. He terrorized us at night, locked us up (sometimes literally) away from our friends and family. He lied, broke promises, broke furniture, broke hearts. That was awful. Yet knowing what others' horrors were and are, how can I possibly feel sorry for myself? Just get over it, Jo.

Jo snaps back to herself.

"Tommy's going to start piano soon." Jo says.

"Oh, wonderful. Is Brian still liking it?" Mama asks.

"He likes it all right. He doesn't really like practicing, but he likes playing what he wants to play."

"Well, that's natural. Boys don't like to be told what to do or when to do it."

"I never much liked it myself, either." Di says.

"He's doing fine. He's developing a lot of other interests, too. He likes basketball. And he's into this video game thing now. It's all the kids talk about at school. Will likes it, too, though he would deny it. It's funny, really, to see him holding the controller and trying not to jump around like the boys do."

Jo takes a breath. She could keep it short and sweet in the courtroom. Talking to her mother was harder than standing in front of a judge.

"I hope they aren't those shooting games with the guns and the women. I'm amazed at what they advertise to children. Even the commercials they show during the day now, they'll give a grown person nightmares. And The Internet. Just a bunch of pedophiles sitting around in dark basements. I hope he's not just following the crowd at school. That's how kids get into trouble." Mama says.

"I like playing poker online. Seems harmless." Di finishes her biscuit.

"Well, Mama, we don't allow him to play those kinds of games. We do realize he's only nine. It's more like racing games, Mario, stuff like that. And the kids aren't allowed online without asking. There are ways to monitor what they can access."

"I was always a Tetris girl, myself." Di says.

"There was a time when you liked basketball." Mama says.

"It was softball. In high school I liked softball." Jo runs her hands up and down the steering wheel, staying in control.

"Oh. I could have sworn it was basketball."

"Nope. It wasn't. I played second base for a year. Finally

realized I wasn't all that great at it. It was actually really disappointing for me."

Di pretends to search for something in her purse.

"I'm sorry I don't remember properly. And now you're angry with me." Mama says.

"No. No need to apologize. I'm not angry," *I'm fucking furious.* "It's fine." But it didn't feel fine. It never felt fine.

Jo glances in the mirror at Mama. She sees her mother's eyes scanning the trees through her window. Jesus, she's unbelievable. She doesn't even know who I am. She doesn't remember I played softball because her brain was on a different planet. She was gone, out of it, completely unaware of anyone else. So, don't try to act like you know because you don't. You weren't there.

God. What is it with me? Why can't I just forgive her?

Jo runs a hand through her hair and looks at her mother in the mirror again. Is this how it's always going to be? I want it to be different. She looks tired. And somehow still lovely. But time isn't going backwards. She's just going to get frailer, thinner. There will come a time when she can't wash her own hair or do her own laundry. Di, won't be far behind. What then? Maybe it'll be dementia. Forget who we all are. Maybe it would just be easier that way. Isn't that how it works? You forget where you are, who your friends are, who your kids are, but keep your long-term memories. Shit. I don't want that for her. What would I do? Beg them to drug her. They probably wouldn't do it. The joke's on you! Just kidding! Turns out time CAN go backward. All those years you spent sewing yourself back together? The forward and back stitches. Yep, it's all coming undone. The threads are breaking because evil is too strong. It's slick with sweat and it bleeds through the seams. It's so fast you can't escape it under this simple, knotted up fabric of you. Did you really think you had it beat? You're so naïve. Daddy's hands on your throat, his spit in your hair. Do you remember? He picks you up and throws you down on the couch sending it slamming, making a dent in the drywall? You throw up, which makes him even madder. David is right there. His diaper is soiled and he screams from a raw rash. Look what you've done to him, he screams at you. I ought to take you right to the police for child neglect, he says. That's what he always did: threatened to take us from you. I pick at that dent for years, pull at the edges of the cracked paint, watch the cracks spread. I dig my fingers into the dusty wall, use my fingernail to carve out a hole. I think one day maybe it'll be big enough for me to crawl into. That dust is still there under my nails. I can't get it out. Can't get away from his jeering, self-satisfied voice -You're never seeing that bitch of a mother again or your whore of a sister, neither. It is the first time he hits me. I'm a little girl, and he hits me. Do you remember it? A blow to the stomach. Feels like someone has thrown a bowling ball at me, but I haven't managed to catch it properly. It hurts to breathe. You scream and start hitting him. He opens the drawer and pulls out a small black gun and tells you to keep on hitting him and see what happens. You scream. Just do it, Ryland, just shoot me because I'd rather be dead! So he decides to point the gun at me instead. I look at the black hole at the end of the gun's barrel.

Jo chews on a fingernail. Her heart is racing and there's a soreness in her chest, the muscles all taught and unforgiving. "I'm going to pull off at this exit for a minute."

Di leans forward. "What's up, chicken butt?"

"Jo, what is it? Are you all right?" Mama is concerned, no, frightened. Everything is so intense.

"I just need to pull off for a minute. Get out of the car." Jo pulls over. The tires bump leaving the pavement. Jo stops abruptly in the grass verge. She grabs for her seatbelt, her fingers are slippery and it takes her an extra second to click the red button. "Just a second. That's all I need."

She gets out, unsteady on her feet. Her limbs are not her own. She walks away from the car. Her nervous energy tells her to walk. She rubs her sweaty hands on her jeans. She's been through this all her life. She was an adult before she knew what to call it. She knows how to cope. She talks to herself. I see trees. I see trucks. I see cars. I see trash on the ground, a cup, some kind of paper. There's a red car, white one, black, red again, blue. A bit later her breathing slows. All right, more control. I smell exhaust. I smell grease. She tells herself she's fine, she's not going to faint. She breathes in and out. She's not going to throw up. She stops and breathes until she feels the panic backing away. Her fingers ball in to fists. She digs her nails into her palms. She opens her hands and then closes them into fists again. Open. Close. Open. Close. Again, she wipes her hands on her pants. She counts her fingers from left to right and then from right to left. And then again. When her breath comes back to her, she turns around and heads back to the car. Di is smoking. FUCK. FUCKING SHIT. I don't want to talk about this. Not right now. She's irritable. Will knew not to approach her when she was like this. She depends on him to know how to deal with her panic attacks. He knows not to say anything, just to stay close. She needs some headroom. The amount of energy and mental focus it takes to get herself out of one of these panics is exhausting.

"You all right? You're pale." Di talks with smoke trailing out of her mouth.

"Yes. And, please, I don't want to talk about it."

Di puts her hands up. "No problem here. You're scaring your Mama, though."

Jo turns on her. "Well, shit, Di. What do you want me to

do? It's not my fault she's scared."

"No, it's not your fault. Not saying it is. Looking for fault, or blame and where it came from, well, that's a story with no seeable beginning, 'cause something is always causing something else. There's never going to be a satisfactory answer for you...what I'm saying is that maybe right now you could smile and say you're fine."

"I am fine. We're all fine. Just like always."

"Bullshit. But okay. Whatever you've got on your mind right now, try to put it aside. This ain't the easiest trip we've ever made. She's doing her best."

"You know what? I think you're probably right. I think this is about the best she can do, because I've certainly seen her at her worst. And I'm a fucking pro at acting like it's all fine. My shit is blue ribbon material."

"Your shit is shit like everyone else's. Just remember something: No matter who a person is, no matter what a person's been through, you can be pissed as hell at your mama, but she's still your mama and *her* mother is in a garbage bag on the floor of the car."

"I know that."

"No, you don't. Cause you haven't lost yours yet."

"Di, I've lost her over and over and over again. How could you forget? You were there every time."

A chilly October breeze blows at their backs. They make their way to the car.

17

Diana

Di gets out for a smoke and watches Jo pace along the side of the road. She finds herself in this same spot time after time; in the middle of mother and daughter, trying to keep the dams from breaking. She feels the waters rising and she's not so sure she's strong enough this time. Or maybe she is, and she just doesn't want to be. She looks back at the car where her sister waits. Another trip to Wimbee. At least this time it's not an escape. This time she's not driving all night...

Di sits, hands clinched on the steering wheel at ten and two, looking over her shoulder every few seconds. Wait...wait...wait...look. Wait...wait...wait...wait...look. My damn hands, she thinks and shakes them to relieve the numbness, ...wait...look. She sees them coming up the street, one walking fast and one running to keep up.

"Damn, girl." Di says as she takes their bags and puts them in the trunk, quietly closing the lid. Catherine opens the door to the back seat and lays David down. Jo opens the opposite door and gets in the back. "I thought he was never coming home."

"Me neither." Catherine is breathless and shiny, sweat making her forehead glow in the light from the streetlamp.

"You good back there, you two rascals?" Di winks at the backseat. She can't see their faces. Their bodies are small on the wide vinyl bench seat. David is curled up and unrecognizable. He is a dark mass. Jo is sitting up, her pale feet slipped into tennis shoes, legs sticking out straight. Di turned around and pulls the car away from the curb. No lights. No radio. Just hot breath and wet skin sticking to the seats.

She grabs a bag of powdered donuts and tosses them back to Jo. "Here you go. Sugar for shug." She hears a small, tired thank you.

"So, where to, young lady?" She grins at Catherine.

"Shut up." Catherine is on edge. Rightfully so, of course, but it's always been her nature anyway. Her skirts always the right length. Her hands always folded nicely in her lap, not like Di's whose fingers were always up to no good. Poking, peaking, prying. Catherine in the department store chooses the "sensible" heel over the platform. She didn't burn her bras, just adjusted the straps and hoisted them up even higher. She wanted what most wanted and some rose up against, fighting tooth and unpainted nail. She wanted to get married, have a family, do the meals and the diapers and the washing and the beach vacations with sunburned noses in the summer and pies and turkeys with dressing and Christmas presents on Christmas morning (like all good Southern Protestants). She wanted the gelatin molds, a microwave, and grapevines painted on the tile backsplash in her kitchen. She wanted a Southern Living subscription and a pitcher meant just for lemonade. No, no, dear. That's the lemonade pitcher. You'll want to put the tea in the other pitcher. The tea pitcher.

How the hell did we end up here? Di stares down the two-lane road, quickly checks the mirror for an angry violent husband driver. Stare...check...stare...stare...check...stare...

"So, did he think anything was up? How was he?"

"His normal self, I guess. I think I did okay. Keep going over it in my head."

Mmhmm, says Di. The mirror, the mirror.

"He's going to know, Di. He'll come. And I don't know how to be strong."

"Hush. It's not going to be like that. No way. Not this time, honey. This is it for sure. No way you're going and taking the kids and a new baby back to that. And you are strong. He's the weak one. Not going back this time. It can't be done. Won't be. I won't let it."

Catherine closes her eyes. Di lets the conversation rest and focuses on the drive. She uses her adrenaline to guide her down the dark roads. It keeps her awake. Nothing is going to creep up on her in the dark. Catherine will go back. She always goes back. He will come and she won't be able to say no. There's nothing I can do but drive.

In the soft light of the morning, Di drives. The children and Catherine in the car sleeping in jolting fits, fear and exhaustion pulling the balance of sleep one way or another, Di drives to her mother's house, the house she and Catherine know, can recall with the scent of salt air or the aroma of Maxwell House coffee or Ritz perfume or burned toast.

Di sees it again:

She opens the oven and smoke from the black toast fills the kitchen. Mama and Catherine in the middle of the living room, in the middle of arguing, in the middle of Di's life. How could you, asks Mama. Because I love him, says Catherine. And he loves me. And we...we...we...And Mama says there will be no we, no way. That boy is rude and doesn't have any kind of sense. I've known his daddy, Bull, all my life and men just like him and, for heaven's sakes, if your daddy were here. And Catherine yells at Mama because Daddy isn't here. Catherine lays it out - Daddy might've been there if Mama hadn't made him sick. What in the hell is that supposed to mean, says Mama. If you'd been nicer, if...you'd just forgiven him. Di is opening windows to let out smoke and says Stop it, y'all. They're going to hear you all the way down at the pier. Di wafts the smoke with a dish towel and Catherine is crying and says Ryland loves me, Mama. It's not his fault his parents are awful! You just want to control me. You ran Hetch off and now you're trying to do the same thing with Ryland and guess what! I DON'T CARE! Catherine runs from the room. Di, you've got to convince her not to go and marry that boy. Mama...I...don't know if I can. No, says Mama, you've got to. If he takes her, we'll never see her again. We'll lose her. Promise me, Di. What, Mama? She'll listen to you. You're her sister. What am I supposed to do, says Di? Her dish towel floats up and down, the grey smoke billows around her.

The cars are rushing by. A transfer truck speeds past, rocks the car from side to side. Di looks up the road at Jo and back at her sister in the car. I tried, I really did. Catherine wouldn't listen. She'd made up her mind about Ryland. I'm sorry, Mama, but you should have been the one to stop her. You never should have asked me to go.

Di exhales, the smoke rises and then quickly blows away as another car passes. Di wants to tell Jo to pull it together, to try harder. She wants to tell Catherine to wake up, to recognize Jo for who she is and what she's been through.

Di wants to hug her mother again.

Di looks up and sees Jo returning to the car. No turning back now.

18

Catherine

Catherine watches Jo and Di yards away, years away.

It was the summer. Jo was eight years old. They were driving down the road with the windows open. Air conditioner didn't work in the car anyway. That didn't matter because their song was on and they were in the middle of the last chorus, the part where they always kicked their singing into high gear. Jo was on her knees in the front seat because kids could still do that kind of thing. She was singing with her eyes closed and her head thrown back, her right arm soaring out the window. David was in the back picking at a scab on his knee. And right then, everything was all okay. Catherine tries to find these moments as she looks back on her life, the moments where she felt like she was being a mother. Jo smiling. Jo laughing. David content in his own world, but not yet hurting anything or anyone; a time when she still had some control over him. She is hungry for these moments, starved of them. There are too few. She plays the ones she has held on to. They are movies in her head.

Both births were complete joy. Sweet David was a gift she

didn't think she'd get. She feared every day she'd lose her baby. Ryland was worse than ever. Drinking, screwing women, lashing out at her. Always at her. The fact that David survived was more evidence of God's glory. She felt the sadness in his baby body and knew she had fed it to him even before he was born. He didn't deserve it and she would be forever apologizing, forever wishing she could take his place in that hospital.

But her first baby was a happy one. Jo, who wouldn't wait and was born on the kitchen floor. She, Catherine, just a twenty-year-old child, was frightened, her back pushed up against the shelves, the phone lying on the floor beside her. Of course she'd called Di. She always called her sister. She wasn't about to call her mother. What could she have done, anyway? But Di didn't make it in time. They were both so young, weren't they? Ryland was out drunk from the night before. There was no one else there. And with a breath and a push, she was no longer alone. The pain didn't matter. She doesn't even remember it. She does remember reaching up and grabbing a dish towel, wrapping her baby in it and being completely and utterly amazed. How is it possible that something this beautiful, this good, this precious came from me? Thank you, God. Those three minutes she spent alone with her baby were the most peaceful of her life. Three minutes. Then the paramedics showed up and so did Di and everyone was so happy. Four days later, Ryland demanded sex, forced himself on her, ripped her stitches. It wasn't the last time she would have to throw out bloody sheets.

She retreats to the memory of the car and their song on the radio. That day they had just arrived home with groceries, put them on the counter and Jo went in the living room to watch TV David was on the floor pulling at the carpet. Even her most precious memories were traveling with demons.

She didn't see the car, but she heard the crunch of the

gravel driveway. A dark car, probably black. Two people. Two police officers, one a woman. One minute Catherine was putting away a bag of rice and the next her life, stiff and cold like ice in a cup, was melted, transformed in front of her at the kitchen table, spilled for everyone to see.

A concerned neighbor called the police, thought they should check in on the family.

Catherine knows:

Made some coffee. Got down two cups. Is your husband Ryland Evans? Are you and your husband having problems? We have some reports of arguing, sounds of a domestic dispute. The male officer asked all the questions. We argue sometimes, she says. Di showed up and What's this about? Where is your husband now, Mrs. Evans? I don't know, which was the truth. His parents are Bullard and Sally Evans? Yes. Could he be there with them? No, he wouldn't go there. Probably passed out at a friend's. He offers pictures to Catherine. Maybe one of these friends? No I don't know them she said without taking the pictures. He shows the pictures again. Not that I know of. Who are they? She asks. He doesn't answer. Does your husband own a gun? Yes. What kind is it, do you know? No... well, it's a handgun. Black. The woman cop smirked. Di stared at her, smiled, inviting her to smirk again. The male officer leaned in, talked low, Does he hurt you, Ma'am? I see some marks on your arm. Get drunk and angry? He turned to look at the kids, hurt them too? Catherine calls to Jo. Jo, take your brother outside, please. Where were you last night? Here with them? Ma'am, I'm real sorry to tell you that we suspect your husband and his friends were involved with the beating of another man. She thinks, Of course he was. She says, My husband? My husband, Ryland? What do you mean? Why? Di motioned for them to stop talking and she went out the door. Catherine saw Di through the screened door talking to Jo. Jo. David. My God. I can't protect them.

19

Jo

The atmosphere for the first hour or so back in the car is polite and stiff. Gradually, everyone settles back in their seats, unclenches their jaws, and releases the tension in their shoulders. Jo listens as the two sisters talk about their neighbor's cat who had snuck inside someone's open car window for a nap. The driver, who returned to the car awhile later, didn't realize the cat was there and drove off.

"Well, damn if that cat didn't jump out from behind the driver's seat right on top of that man's bald head. The cat was scratching and hissing and you could see the car weaving through the parking lot, the man looking like he was wearing Daniel Boone's hat and was not happy about it." Di laughed and slapped her thigh.

"Di, you are full of exaggerations." Mama says.

"What? It's all true. You can ask Renee. She saw it, too."

"Renee? I wouldn't believe her if the sky were charcoal gray and she claimed it was going to rain. You know she's the one that spread all those rumors about the last manager, Cliff, I think it was, that he was fooling around with that teenage girl in the B building. He wasn't here two weeks before the HOA committee had him shipped out."

"But was it true?" Jo asks.

"What true?"

"Was Cliff messing around with a teenage girl?"

"Well, I don't know. But it didn't seem like something Renee ought to be talking about. Leave that up to the girl's parents, is how I see it. It's a family issue. That girl didn't need everybody talking about her." Mama says.

"Renee is observant." Di says. "She pays attention, which is a lot more than can be said for most people."

Mama shakes her head. "She's a busy-body who likes drama."

"Well, she doesn't have much else to do, really."

"Sounds like the girl's parents did have something to say about it." Jo says. "And they got him fired or transferred. If it was true, I hope they pressed charges."

Mama looks out the window. "What good would that do? The damage was already done."

Through her rearview mirror, Jo sees her mother's white hair shine in the sun.

It's the tunnel. Every visit to Wimbee the drive through the tunnel created by the magnificent Southern live oak trees fascinates Jo. The oaks are sturdy with trunks, thick and steadfast. The branches droop, curve, twist, and lift to reach across the narrow road to their sisters on the opposite side.

These are moments Jo feels transported from the harsh light and cold realities of the known world to a safer realm. Who could not be attracted to it, caught in the spell of the Spanish moss draping, dangling and possibly whispering among the branches? She loves this shadowed drive, has always loved it. As a child she suspected the trees were witches with unkempt, enticing hair, and hoped they were good witches to be trusted. Now Jo's witches that lined the road have morphed into enduring ladies with their hair hanging loose and flowing.

Because some of the strong branches dip down toward the ground and then spread out wide, Jo had some times climbed and hid among the oak trees. She'd watch the road below to make certain she couldn't be seen. When she felt her secret place was undetected, she with delicate touches, combed through the moss.

The moss is its own plant, separate from the oak tree. The plant finds the trees it likes and attaches itself, feeding and growing off the tree's nutrient supply. Sometimes it grows thick and lush because of the tree's fertile life source, but the moss then turns on the tree, keeps it from growing as big as it should and in some rare cases, kills it. She'd learned that from a book at Bibba's house.

Bibba's house.

Jo was through the tunnel and ahead they would cross the bridge to the island. She'd prepared herself the best she could, but it is THE bridge. Jo sees over the sides down to the water. She knows better than to look, but she does look. That's crazy. She knows it is, but she can't help it. She hates all bridges over water and tries to keep her mind on driving toward solid ground. She picks a spot ahead and focuses on getting closer and closer to it. No matter how hard she tries to keep it away, the memory flashes at her. She blinks quickly to wash away the terrible sight of her father's body floating there facedown. Wait. Was that his arm moving! He swims to the shore, runs up the bank and chases her car. She presses down on the gas pedal. *How long is this bridge?*

A brief nightmare. His body was never floating in the water. There was a storm that day on the bridge. She can feel her hair wet and stringy, hanging in front of her eyes while he holds the gun to her head. It was so stormy, the current was fast, the water choppy. There were no fishermen in the water. No witnesses to where his body fell.

She focuses her eyes on the road ahead. Di and Mama haven't said a word. They are keepers of their own thoughts.

When they reach the other side, there's a shift in the air, in her body, in time. They pass a lone loblolly pine in an expanse of marsh. The tree is her distance marker. She has made it over the bridge. Her hands relax on the wheel. She becomes that girl again, the one she remembers as if the girl is someone separate from herself. A little girl she knew once. A girl, who, if she saw her now in her pink shorts and lavender shirt, ponytail, white tennis shoes, she, the adult Jo, would want to approach cautiously. Kneel on the ground, arms wide open, inviting the girl, begging the girl to come to her, to be safe with her, to be loved, to tell that child she is good and kind and smart and brave and that she doesn't have to worry because it will all be okay.

"What happened to the Pig?" asks Mama.

"Bi-Lo bought out Piggly Wiggly down here a couple of years ago, Mama."

"Doesn't seem right."

"It's not all that different on the inside. You still got to pay island prices for a tube of toothpaste." Jo says.

Di asks if they should stop now or just go on to the house.

Both Mama and Jo agree to stop now, neither of them wanting to hurry anything along.

"Lord, please don't let me see anyone I know." Mama says.

"You could always put a bag over your head. I'll lead you around, if you want." Jo laughs. "Oh, come on. It'll be okay. We'll keep our heads low and be in and out real quick."

Di volunteers to stay with the car.

"Maybe I could stay with the car, too," Mama asks.

"Nope. Not getting out of it. I don't know what you want. You have to come."

They don't need much. Some bread, milk, coffee, butter, ham, cheese, eggs, grits, bacon. Jo picks out a couple bottles of wine.

"Do we really need two bottles?" Mama eyes Jo.

"Yes, Mama."

They weave the buggy through the narrow aisles. Jo tries to squeeze past displays of baked beans and racks of spice packets. Mama holds on to the side of the cart making it more difficult for Jo to steer. Mama turns to face Jo.

"I recognize that woman."

"What? You're whispering. I can't hear you."

Mama shyly gestures to a woman at the end of the aisle. The woman was short and standing on her tip-toes trying to read the label on a can. "I think I know her."

"Oh. Okay. What do you want me to do? I can't turn around.—Oh, shit. She just looked at me."

"Is she coming?"

Jo smiled. "She's coming, she's coming toward us. Turn around and say something. Now."

Mama's eyes briefly close before she turns around. The woman has a bright face, welcoming. She's probably Mama's age, maybe a little older and wears a bright blue sweatshirt with WIMBEE written across the front in white letters. She's plump and cute.

"Catherine? Is that you? Yes! Hello!"

"Oh, my goodness. Hello. So good to see you. You remember my daughter? Josephine?"

Jo realizes Mama doesn't remember this woman's name. Jo waves. "Hi, I'm Jo. I'm sorry. Have we met? I can't seem to place your name."

The woman smiles. "Oh, well, you wouldn't, would you? You were so young. I'm Fran Dowling. I knew your mother when we were kids, but I moved away when I got married. But, now I'm back. We all seem to come back for one reason or another, don't we? Oh, Catherine. I was so sorry to hear about your mother passing."

Mama breathes, her relief showing in her face, which Fran may have mistaken for resignation to her loss, but Jo knew it to be something more complicated than that. Mama had passed the first test of coming home. She thanked Fran for her condolences.

Fran's husband died two years ago and her children were off raising their own families. She came home.

"I don't know. I just missed being near the water. I have such wonderful memories of this place. I thought, why not?" Her cheeks are rosy even under the fluorescent lights.

Jo helps Fran reach the can of reduced sodium peas, they say their goodbyes and part ways. Maybe running into the past wouldn't be too hard.

Mama turns to Jo. "I think we need a pie."

Back at the car, Jo stuffs the receipt and coupons down into her purse and looks across the street where she and Bibba used to shop sometimes. After that day her daddy showed up, after all that mess, Jo, Mama, David, and Di lived on Wimbee Island with Bibba. *Just for a while,* her Mama would say. *For as long as you need,* Bibba would say. Jo rode with Bibba everywhere. Helped with the groceries, volunteered with Bibba at the library after school, anything to not go back to Bibba's. It got easier after a time.

She looks at her mother as she gets in the car. "You think Nadine is still in there selling her shell earrings?"

Mama sighs. "Lord knows those were the ugliest earrings. They looked like something you'd get out of a gum-ball machine."

"They weren't even shells. They were pieces of shells glued to plastic. Looked like baby teeth to me," laughed Di.

"I will never forget when Bibba and I ran into Nadine at The Pig." Jo says. They all know this story, have heard it hundreds of times, but it doesn't matter. It's part of the remembering.

"Nadine was such a nosey gossiper and she said something rude about Hetch and Bibba asked her why didn't she go hot glue some of her Goddamned shell earrings. Best moment of my childhood. I will never ever forget that." Jo is shaking her head and smiling. She can still see Nadine's face.

"She was such a bitch." Mama says and Di and Jo howl because when Mama curses it sounds like a child trying it out for the first time.

"That was the summer that Hetch taught me to swim in the ocean." Jo says as she lowers her window to smell the air. It takes only half a second to realize which summer she was thinking of, which makes her regret mentioning it, but the memory of swimming with Hetch is a happy one.

His dark hair, long arms and legs. His tan skin was wet and shiny in the sun, like he was covered in beautiful jewels. She thinks how big his hands had seemed to her then. And how she wasn't afraid of them. After Daddy was gone, Hetch showed up at the house. She feels what she often felt as a child, of wanting to run to him, to crawl in his pocket and hide. Take me with you. Stay here with me. I can't take care of her on my own. It's just all so much and I don't know how to fix it. Jo now knows what her child-mind couldn't process: her mother's grief, sadness, depression. What she did see as a child was that Mama was better when Hetch was around. She was calmer, didn't get upset as easily. He could get her to eat. And that was enough. It was like there was an invisible rope tied around her waist and every time she tried to walk off the end of the earth, Hetch pulled her back. She wished Mama would hug him. Put your arms around him, Mama. Don't let him go. Don't make him go.

They drive down the main road and pass the houses she has known forever. There are a few new ones with names like "The Shark Shack" and "Beach Blessed." But the same college flags fly. The University of South Carolina Gamecocks' colors, black and garnet and white climb the flagpoles. Clemson University orange and purple and white clash across the street. Neighbors hoisting their flags higher and higher, trying to outdo the guy next-door. The occasional Michigan or Maryland fan tries to jump in, but nothing beats this homegrown rivalry.

They pass the marina on the right. On sunny afternoons, Di used to walk Jo and David down to the store there and buy ice cream cones, thumb through magazines, and try on beach hats. They would sit at the picnic tables and watch the fishing boats pull up to the dock. The seagulls and beach birds haunted the parking lot waiting to fight over whatever was thrown out after the boats were cleaned and gassed up.

The sun is beating down and Jo is licking the chocolate river from her hand. Di tugs at the little girl's hat to better cover her small face.

"You better eat quicker," laughs Di.

Jo smiles. "I like it here."

"Yeah? What do you like?"

"I like watching the boats come in."

"Maybe you could be a fisherwoman one day. Have your own
boat."

"Girls don't do that."

"Why?"

"Well, I've never seen one do it. All these are men."

"Yeah, well. It always starts that way, but it doesn't mean you can't be the first one around here." Di pauses and wipes David's face. "What would you name your boat?"

Jo's face turns thoughtful. She looks around at the other boat names. The Good Life, Sea Ya, 401K, and Jean Marie.

"It doesn't have to be clever. You can name it anything you want," Di says.

Di turns, straining against her seatbelt and points at the marina. "Remember your boat name, Jo?"

"Uh...yes, I do, actually."

"The Catherine," Di whispers.

Jo sees the sign on the mailbox. The words are hard to read now. The paint is cracked and chipped. She slows to pull into the driveway of Bibba's house. A few months back, right after Bibba died, Jo came to the house to check on things, to clean out the fridge, turn off the water. And to cry. To cry and cry, and moan her Bibba's name, to say it out loud, to wish for her, to curse her, to love her, to remember her. It was exhausting.

Will told her to go alone. At first, she felt like he was sending her away, but when she got there and after she purged herself of her Bibba's name, she knew why he had done it. He had known what she needed. And isn't that love? He does love me, she had said to herself. And cried again.

When she came alone, she found herself driving past Bibba's driveway, not ready to pull in, not ready to go anywhere. She drove down the street and parked near one of the familiar posts with a blue number twelve painted on it. Public Access Bridge Twelve. She slipped off her shoes and stepped into the sand. She walked down to the water. The waves were calm and the skies clear of clouds. A shrimp boat sat on the horizon and she wondered how far away it was.

How far do you have to go to sit on the edge of the Earth, your legs dangling over the side into nothingness or whatever is after all this? And if you were to get a glimpse of what's beyond and you had to choose, would you stay? Her stomach growled.

She made her way back to the access bridge, back to the car, and back past Bibba's. The girl ran with her car. Purple shorts and pink shirt, ponytail swaying. Jo pulled into the parking lot of Shealey's Seafood and looked in her rearview. The girl stood, hands on hips, staring back. Jo walked through the gravel lot, turning back only once to make sure the girl was gone, and then went through the door of the restaurant. The smell of fried everything hit her. The cheery hostess beamed. Jo was surprised the pretty girl was old enough to earn a paycheck let alone chew gum, but apparently she was. Jo pointed toward the bar and the hostess nodded. She sat at a two-seater bar table. After the waiter took her order of a glass of the house chardonnay (no need to splurge) and a sloppy cheeseburger, she looked around and saw that the decor hadn't changed much. Not at all, actually. The crabbing nets and buoys still hung on the walls. The gigantic chandelier made of oyster shells was hanging in the main room over the tables with holes cut in the middle. If a person didn't grow up or visit a seaside town, he might not know about the trash cans that sat underneath those holes to catch the debris of a hungry patron. Crab shells, oyster shells, shrimp legs, half-eaten hushpuppies and the like. Jo looked at the squeeze bottle of tartar sauce sitting on her table and thought that might be an original, too. She slid it to the far end.

"Jo Evans?"

Oh. God. Not today.

"Hey, girl!"

Jo looked over and couldn't help but smile. Lisa walked

over in her Carolina t-shirt and cut-off jean shorts looking just like herself even though it had been years.

"Don't you age?" Jo gets up to hug her.

"Lord, you know you're the one. Just look at you. Fancy girl."

"You are so full of it. Still."

"Well, somebody has to be. Otherwise, we'll all die of boredom around here." She motions to a group of her friends at the end of the bar. "You want to join us?"

"No, thanks. I'm fine. I just needed to eat something. Not staying long.

"You here on account of Bibba."

"Yeah. I have to go to her place and have a look around."

Lisa sits across from Jo. Her face is thoughtful and kind, just like it's always been. After it all, that day at school, when the principal showed up and called her name, after the bridge and the police station and the hospital, days of crying, nights of dying, Lisa came and sat with Jo out on the porch. She didn't ask many questions, just enough. On the weekends, she came around lunch time and Bibba fixed them both egg salad sandwiches with chips and pickles on the side. They peeled oranges while sitting on the beach, Aunt Di sitting a few yards behind them. Jo went down to the hair salon with Lisa and helped her sweep up what was cut and left on the floor. Lisa's mother was quiet, but nice. She kept her space neat and tidy, especially when the girls were there to help. When the day came for Jo to return to school, Lisa held her hand and they went in together.

"So?" Lisa looks at Jo.

"So..."

"It's been awhile. I know you're married. Two kids?"

Jo smiles. "Three. All boys."

"Shit."

"Yep."

They laugh and Jo catches her up on life and Will and the kids. Lisa works at the dentist's office. She's divorced with a daughter who is about to graduate high school and then leaves for college next fall.

"Honestly, Jo. I can't believe it. I didn't screw her up. She wants to be a nurse. She's good at taking care of people."

"I can believe it. You took care of me."

"You took care of yourself. I was just there in case it wore you out."

Thoughts are left unsaid as they can be between friends that have seen each other's darkness.

Lisa cocks her head. "You staying at the house?"

"Oh, no. I've got a hotel for tonight. Going back in the morning."

"I was guessing as much. You need company? Got a lot of stuff to move out?"

"Thanks, Lisa. I'm good. I really came to see what needs to be done. Not planning on cleaning anything out yet."

Lisa has to go and Jo's burger arrived, so good timing they say. They hug and tears fill Jo's eyes. She knows Lisa sees them and won't acknowledge them, which makes it harder to hold them back. It's the small understandings that can unravel everything.

After her burger and one more chardonnay, Jo sat on the porch steps wondering if she would make it inside. She stood and took the few steps up the stairs. The porch column on the left was replaced by Hetch, probably. She hadn't ever thought of that before. But of course it would be him. He would have carefully taken down the scarred wood, cut and sanded and painted a new one. That's what he did after all, fixed things. What's funny, though, is that even the replacement column, the new and pretty, was a reminder of the old and scarred simply by being.

She was worried about where her mind would go without the distraction of company. Thoughts of her father coated everything like dust. He was in the walls under the new coats of paint, ground into the floor, into the crevices. She knew she had to do it. She did, finally, and realized it hadn't killed her. And she was so glad she had because as she was going through some of Bibba's things, she found a stack of letters. They looked like something you would see in an old war movie. Blue and red stripes were printed along the border of the envelopes. The handwriting on each letter was the same as the one before. All to the same person, her mother Catherine. The return address was an APO. She wasn't sure. No, she was sure. She knew they were all from Hetch. And they were unopened. She fingered the seal on one envelope. So small and formal, like little presents. She knew at once that she'd found something significant, a secret Bibba was keeping. Why? Why would you do this, Bibba? Jo struggled not to open them. They weren't for her, though. She put them in her bag and wondered what to do next. Is it better to let sleeping letters lie?

So now all three of Bibba's girls are here. Jo pushes down the parking break. "Y'all give me a sec. I'm just going to grab the mail before we go up." Keep it together. She tells herself. It's dizzying to stand in the same spot where, as a child, you hid, thinking that your mother was dead, strangled to death, thrown through a window, punched so hard her teeth were coming out the back of her head. The same sign on the same mailbox on the same post in the same dirt by the same trees. This is the spot where she crumbled. She was eight again, running from school all the way back to the house because she knew her father was there, had found them somehow. It's okay. You couldn't have done anything. She says to her eight year old self. You froze. You were terrified. No wonder you peed your pants. The monster was close. And then she saw Hetch's face, so close to her face calling her name, shaking her by the shoulders. How many times has she relived all of it?

Jo's phone rings. She looks at the screen and realizes she's not breathing. She takes a deep breath before answering.

"Hi."

"Hey, there. How's it going? Y'all there yet?" Will's voice. She felt the blood moving in her veins again. She wishes she were holding his hand.

She clears her throat. "Just got here. How was school? Did the boys have a good day?" There are a few bills, but mostly junk in the mailbox. She tosses it all in the passenger seat and turns to Di and Mama. She mouths "Will" and they nod.

"Oh, you know. Middle schoolers love learning U.S. History about as much as the Native Americans do. Decided to put on a documentary so they could nap and I could get some grading done."

"Pop quiz on Monday?"

"You know it."

"That'll show 'em."

"Hey, did you mean to send me a text of an eggplant and a tomato?"

Jo's cheeks are hot. "Oh. Yes. I, well, was trying to send you a fun message. Tomato? I thought I sent a peach. To make you think of me while I'm gone."

"Oh, that's cute, babe."

Jo feels his smile. She hears her sons in the background, specifically, Tommy and Matt arguing.

"Have you shown her the letters yet?"

Jo glances in the review mirror. "No, not yet. I'll probably do it later once we're settled." Would she?

"Right. Okay. Well, we're leaving in a few to go visit with my dad.

"Oh, good. I know he'll love that."

"Yeah, things have been good lately. He's genuinely trying with the kids."

"He loves them, Will. He loves you, too, you're just not a kid anymore like they are."

"Yeah, I know. Hold on. The boys want to say 'hello.'"

"MOM. Dude. Dad made me a ham and cheese sandwich today. FOR LUNCH...stop, Matt! It's not your turn!" Tommy yelled into the phone.

"Hi, honey! Is that a bad thing? The ham and cheese?"

"No, except he made it with the brown bread and you know I don't like the brown bread. When are you coming home?"

"Oh, well I'm sure it wasn't all that bad. Probably tomorrow. I miss you. Did you have a good day?"

"Okay. Here's Matt."

"MAMA."

"YES, sweet boy?"

"I was wanting to talk to you and Tommy wouldn't let me. We're getting ready to go to Grandpa's."

"You're talking to me now. So, everything is okay. How are you doing? Are you excited to go see Grandpa?"

"Why can't I see you on the phone? Fine. Did you know that I am eating a banana?"

"No, but that sounds good. Honey, the connection out here at the beach is a little slow, so that's why we can't see each other. I love you, Matty."

"I love you too, Mommy."

Matt pushes the big red button and hangs up the phone before Jo can ask to speak with Brian. She tries calling back but no one answers. Matt is probably running around with the phone, a half-eaten banana abandoned on the table. She'll try them again later. Truth is, she can't bear Brian's sigh right now. That sound in his voice that he doesn't want to talk to her. She wants to hear his happiness, his sweetness, his love for her. God, why can't I just be calm about this? It's not even about me. He doesn't hate me. He's just growing up. It's fine.

Jo parks in the same spot they always did. The Cadillac sits under the house as if Bibba were home. Jo can hear the screen door slam and Bogue bark, his nails scrambling on the front porch so he can run down the stairs to meet her. But, no. The door stays closed and there is no wet, black nose sniffing at the handle of the car door. Jo makes a mental note to start the car to make sure it still runs.

Mama and Di walk up the front steps of the house. They pause at the screen door. Mama touches the rocking chair and it moves back and forth. There's a ghost in that chair. Bibba rocked Jo in that chair. Bibba led her through the nightmares, held her hand while she cried, taught her to own her fears. She did all the things Jo's mother couldn't because Jo's mother was broken.

Jo unlocks the door and the three of them enter the house. Di reaches and turns on the lamp on a table near the door. And here they are. The refrigerator hums and newly made ice falls into the freezer bin. The crashing sound startles the women.

"For heaven's sake," says Mama.

They turn on all the lights and open windows. The curtains flutter lightly as the air travels through the house. The clean fresh sea air Jo hadn't realized she misses until now revives the house, giving movement and life to the stale and dusty things that occupy it, the stuff that hasn't been touched or dealt with. They put away groceries. Jo watches the two women, at home here, which is strange, she thinks. So much awfulness has happened here. Aren't they afraid? Don't they share her uneasiness? The memories, the visions. How do they come back here? Jo feels like she's going to retch.

Mama bends over to go through the canned goods at the bottom of the pantry, moving beans, and corn, tomato soup, fruit cocktail. Di makes a pot of coffee. She reaches to get three cups.

"GODDAMN!" Di yells and they all jump and scream, Mama hits her head on the pantry doorknob, a coffee cup crashes to the floor.

"What!" Yells Jo.

"There's a goddamned mouse in here!"

Mama is rubbing her head. "Sweet Jesus, Diana! I could have a concussion with you yelling like that. Here's the broom."

"Look. He was in there waiting on me to grab a cup so he could jump out at me with his mousey fangs. What in the hell am I going to do with a broom?"

"There it is!" Jo points to a gray blur scurrying across the counter.

"Oh, no you don't, sucker." Di whacks the counter, misses the mouse.

"You're an idiot." Mama says.

"You're the one that handed me this damn thing." Di holds up the broom.

Mama shushes Di. They stand still watching for movement.

Mama whispers, "Maybe we scared him off."

After several moments of nothing, Jo grabs her car keys.

"Okay. I'm going to run up and grab some mouse traps."

"No, just...here. Let me go. I need a cigarette and maybe some new underwear." Di hands Jo the broom, takes the keys and her wallet. Jo and Mama hear Di muttering goddamn mouse and something about having a stroke as she goes down the front steps. Mama looks at Jo and they both laugh so hard they have to sit down. Jo hears Bibba's voice saying, all that laughing's going to turn to crying.

Mama cleans up the broken cup. Jo takes down the dishes from the cabinets because who really wants to eat from dishes covered in mouse footprints and whatever else. They both watch for whiskers hoping they've scared him away for the time being.

"That's about all I can fit for now." Jo closes up the dishwasher and bends down to pick the right setting. ON seems to be it. Like everything else in this house, the appliances were new at one time. The saltwater continued to eat away at the washer and dryer. The TV is hooked up to a VHS/DVD player combo. There is no microwave. Bibba didn't believe in microwaves. The couch and armchair in the living room are covered in that large floral print with striped accent pillows stuffed in the corners and creases, the places where people rested their backs and propped their arms and didn't bother to fluff the life back into them. Bibba would never wear patterns like these but she would sit on them. It's like having a garden inside, she would say, and these flowers don't die.

Jo watches her mother wiping off the counter. "Mama."

"Yes?"

"Mama. Does it bother you to be here? At this house?"

"Does it bother you, Jo?"

"Mama, I'm asking you."

"I know. I'm just tired of thinking about how I feel. I'd rather hear about you."

"Well, it's hard, Mama." Jo says. "I can't walk in here without seeing Daddy's face. There are a lot of dark corners here."

Mama nods. She runs her hand over the top of the kitchen table, her fingers barely brushing the surface. "It's hard for me, too. You remember I didn't come back and visit much. That's why Bibba would drive to us. But being here now...this is the same table I ate at as a child, did you know that?"

Jo considers what she knows about her mother's childhood. She remembers a black and white picture of two little girls both in matching summer dresses, white ankle socks, and black, what Mama would call "Sunday" shoes. They are sisters. Their postures are similar. Their eyes squint in the sun. She imagines those two girls sitting at the table in front of her, only she still sees them in black and white. "I guess I hadn't thought about it."

"I sat here and Di sat there." She points at two ends of the table. "Bibba and Daddy were here and here. This place is a number of things to me. I grew up here. I remember my daddy in these rooms. He was a good man, Jo. He tried, he really did. I know he wasn't perfect. He made a lot of mistakes, broke Bibba's heart and ours. Lord. When he died, I don't know. It felt wrong for the sun to rise the next day. He wasn't here anymore, so why should things go on like always? When I look around this house, I see him, us. He put in these cabinets when Bibba wanted new ones. Cussed the entire time he was working. Put on a big show of how difficult it was. Bibba would just roll her eyes."

"Di and I had a tire swing in the tree out back. You can still see where the rope wore a groove into the branch." Mama smiled. "There is a special spot in our old bathroom. If you open the cabinet door on the vanity, there is a small shelf up under the lip of the sink. Di used to hide cigarettes in there. I was loved in this house, Jo. But, it's also where Bibba and I had some of our worst arguments. And it's the place I thought you all would be safe. I was wrong, of course. And, you're right. Those memories are here, too, in the walls, the floors, the dirt in the yard."

"Why did you always go back to him?" Jo releases the words.

She hadn't thought this through. Didn't know she was

going to ask or that she even wanted to know the answer. It's as if her chest pushed up and the words just came out. They'd been lodged in there, weighty, and now they were out in the room, slamming into Mama's face. It's not like she'd never asked before. She had when she was younger and more impulsive and focused on the injustices of the world. Back when she hadn't lived enough life to understand the fuzzy areas. At the time it felt like she'd lived enough for an entire life and more. She was angry when she was younger. She could feel it in her arms and legs. It started in her stomach and crept along her nervous system, following the path that God engineered. The anger and terror and sadness and confusion lived in her fingernails and eyelashes. It was under her tongue and pushing at the back of her eyes, making them feel swollen and heavy. Yes, she had asked or demanded. Why did you let him treat us that way? She thought the question wasn't hard. She thought things were either right or wrong, truths or lies. It's simple: you either survived something or you didn't. But love isn't simple.

"Mama." Jo watches her mother sweep tiny ceramic pieces into the dust pan. The tiniest of pieces, slivers, almost imperceptible to the eye.

And now? She is still angry. She's tried hard at it being less so, and it's working; she isn't blinded by anger anymore while also understanding that some feelings are here to stay.

Because it's not over. But she is calm and she loves her mother.

"Mama?" Jo asks again.

Mama sits in her old spot at the table. "Let me ask you something, Jo. Why do you think you went into the lake that day?"

Jo's stomach lurches. There are a lot of things she and her mother haven't discussed. She never wanted to talk about the lake. Even in therapy sessions, it took her two years to talk openly about it. Talking with her mother about her darkest personal moment was not just hard, it seemed almost impossible.

She sees David throw the stick. She sees his mouth moving, but can't hear his voice. Doesn't matter. She knows what he said, what she did. She remembers the muddy bottom of the lake giving way under her feet and how, as she walked deeper, she had to twist her hips left and right to propel herself through the water. It was so cold. Her teeth were vibrating in her head. Her whole body shook. She saw the stick just a few feet in front of her. The water rose to her shoulders. She reached out for the stick and then saw it in her hands, but she couldn't feel it there. Everything was so cold. Had she made up her mind? Was there a specific moment when she decided not to turn back? She felt herself slip the rest of the way under. Her hair, darker than the water, hovered in front of her and she thought about jellyfish at the beach and Spanish moss and her mother's golden hair in the sunshine. Her father was there reaching for her, his body blue from the cold, his eyes cloudy and dead, and his mouth open, fish swimming in and out. But she wasn't scared because it was obvious he was dead. If she stayed under where she could see his lifeless body, she wouldn't have to be afraid.

Jo brushes her hair back from her shoulders. "I think I was a child. I think...I just can't remember deciding to go under. I wasn't thinking suicidal thoughts, Mama. It wasn't like that. I wasn't thinking about dying. I felt like maybe I could stay there, not come up and it would be okay because, well, it felt safe. It wasn't until after, when I woke up in the hospital and realized I wasn't in the lake anymore, that's when I knew. I knew I'd rather be in the lake where nothing hurt." She wipes the tears from her cheeks.

Mama's eyes are closed. Her hands are up in front of her face as if she is praying. "I cannot describe what it is like to

Alissa C. Miles

hear your child..." she pauses, swallowing hard, "To hear your child who was once a part of you, say she'd rather be drowning in a lake than be living. Out of all the things I have been through, that was the worst. You may not believe that. But it's true."

Jo thinks of her own children and her chin trembles as the tears fall. She reaches for a napkin and hands one to her mother.

Mama wipes her eyes. "Why did I go back to him? Are you asking me this because you want to know if I love you?"

"I know you love me."

"No. You don't. How could you? How could you believe that I love you and David if I would put y'all through that? My children? So, that *is* what you are asking me. You need to know and I'm afraid that there's nothing I can say that won't sound empty. I have always loved you. You know that love, that crazy insane love, you're a mother, you know that love. I see you look at your boys and I wish I could go back and have you see me look at you like that—that fullness, pride, deep deep connection and love. I felt it. I felt it so much that it scared me. Jo, I know it's hard to imagine wanting to be with a man like your father. But he was once a boy in this town, a child like the rest of us. He was hollowed out early on. He was beaten, worked-over by his daddy every day, made into a *man* by someone who didn't know what the word meant. And his poor mother. Sally never was allowed to leave that backwater house. It was a prison. But he survived and it made him hard and cold and his heart and his head were full of fire. On the outside, it made him seem like the daredevil, the bad-boy and that seemed fun at first. And he was very good-looking. While on the inside he was dying to hurt someone, to share his hurt, to not be alone with his rage. And I let myself be that person. At first, he was sweet and fun and told me I was gorgeous, told me there was no one else in the world like me. God, I ate it up. And then, over time, he convinced me that I deserved to be the person he hurt. I'm not making excuses for him. I'm just trying to tell you how it was. It's so hard to explain, honey. The choices I made. There was a short time where I thought I was happy. But now I know I never really was except when you and David were born. Y'all made everything worth it."

Mama stops talking. The dust pan sits between them. Jo is pressing small ceramic shards on the table, mashing them into the table, pressing so hard that her finger, ringed in white and red, will become part of the wood, everything becoming a part of everything else, melding, connecting.

Mama continues.

"When we escaped here that summer, in this house... I grew up in this house, but it didn't feel like it. When we came here, I felt like I was someone different. I'd changed. I wasn't me. I didn't have the energy to be the girl I used to be. It seemed too hard to get back to her. It was something I'd never felt before. But when you have someone telling you how worthless you are over and over and beating you down, breaking you down, me, my children, I became so unsure of myself. I knew what he was capable of. I didn't trust my own mind. It was like a sickness. I lost the baby and my mind was everywhere and nowhere, Jo. I am ashamed to say that I felt relief knowing that I wasn't going to have to let another child go through what y'all had lived through. It's incredibly hard to admit that. I had all these competing feelings and I didn't know what to do with them. Watching you and Hetch play on the beach. You bloomed. And the whole time I knew that it wouldn't last. I had a foot in heartache and another foot in real joy. It was an exhausting way to be."

"And then he was here. Your daddy showed up with this meanness, hatefulness like he'd chewed on the Devil himself, swallowed him whole and I allowed myself to say, 'I'd rather die.' And I would have if it meant it could all be over for us. I even hoped for it. Prayed for it. I knew standing out by that truck, right out there in the driveway, that Hetch, if he had the chance, would kill Ryland. He said as much. Told Ryland he'd never know what hit him. He'd be dead before he hit the ground."

"I wanted Ryland to take me and end it. I didn't want anyone else I loved to become a part of the madness we were living. I was thinking, I'll just go. I'll tell him I'll go with him and he can do whatever he wants to me, just let the kids stay here. Please let the kids stay here. You don't want them. Just me. Just you and me. We'll end this together. I was ready to say goodbye to you and David, if it meant you'd be safe. But I was so stupid to think he would do that. And he was so furious that we'd run away again. Told me I'd humiliated him. How it looked like he couldn't control his wife. So, he was going to show me how he could. And then with the police there and Hetch, everything was getting so bad so quick. I had to decide. I should have told you to run. But I couldn't think straight. Jo, I wasn't strong enough to live without you. And that was always his threat. That he would hurt you, get rid of you, make you disappear. I couldn't let that happen. He pointed that gun at your head and I couldn't think clearly. It changed everything. I just wanted you with me. It was selfish. I know that. I shouldn't have let him put you in that truck. You were my life-line. I'm alive, Jo, because of you and David. And I was absent for a time. I know it seemed like I didn't care. I hurt you and I can hardly stand it. I'm the one that made you walk into that lake. I can't tell you how sorry I am for that."

Mama touches the fingers of her right hand to her forehead, covering her face for a minute. She is trembling.

Jo reaches out her hand. "No, it wasn't your fault. It was his. You're not selfish, Mama."

"But it was. And then I went numb. After he came to the house, I don't know. It's like I jumped off that bridge, too. I couldn't feel the ground underneath me. I was here but I wasn't. I'm so sorry, Jo. I don't know how to explain it."

Jo doesn't know what to say. Her mother's apology, which she knows is sincere, falls heavily on her heart. "It's okay. It was terrible for all of us. I struggle sometimes, knowing what to say or when I think back to the time you missed with us, but that's because you're my mother and I love you. I want you to know I made it. Look at me here and see that I've done well. You're a part of that. There are times when I'm overwhelmed by all we've been through. But we did get through."

Sometimes what seems impossible seems so because it is clouded by hurt, and when that hurt is moved aside, not gone, just shifted, the impossible is seen more clearly, seen for what it truly is: something possible.

Jo wonders if now is the right time. "Mama, I have something to show you. Something I found." She goes to her purse and pulls out the stack of letters. "Now might not be right, but, sit down, Mama. I think you deserve to see these."

Mama stares at the letters. Before she can turn the first one over, the door opens and Di walks in. "Never guess who I ran into." She says holding the door open. Di winks at Jo and shrugs as if to say *What?! It just happened!*

He walks in, skin tan even in the fall. All Mama can do is whisper. *Hetch.*

Bibba

November 5, 2014

There is something else I want you to try and remember. After everything happened and your mother was unable to care for you and David, that was not a choice, it was truth. It was vulnerability. I know you needed her. But we did okay, didn't we? Diana, Hetch and I? We tried the best we could, Diana especially. Of course, when she sets her mind to something, she can be quite bullish. But she always errs on the side of love. Diana would have been a great mother, you know?

P.S. See if you can get her to quit smoking.

20

Catherine

Catherine looks down at the letters. She looks up at Hetch.

"Did you at least remember the mouse traps?" Jo asks.

Di holds up a bag. "And some sub sandwiches."

"Sounds like you've got a mouse problem." Hetch says.

Jo smiles. "Well, would you really expect anything less from us?"

Ha! says Di and Hetch is laughing his Hetch laugh. Jo hugs him, his arms wrapping around her with real intent. Not one of those barely-there hugs. It was a sincere hold, her head resting on his chest. He is still tall, but his shoulders don't seem quite as broad. His step has a little less bounce. But his eyes are shining and his smile is big and welcoming.

Catherine looks him over from head to toe. He is Hetch, but she is surprised by his age. When she is folding laundry, doing the dishes, taking a walk, reading a book, the moments when she is calm and her mind is resting, his image visits her, but not this image. The image is young and she feels relieved to see him like this, like her.

"I don't understand." Is all Catherine can manage to say.

She is holding the letters. She looks at Jo and Di. "Did you plan this?"

"No, no. Well, I did plan on giving you the letters, but I didn't know Hetch would be here." Says Jo.

"You forget how small this island is?" Di asks.

Catherine sets the envelopes on the table. Hetch glances at them. He offers to set out the traps. She knows her hair is a mess, and she's been crying. No doubt, she looks old and worn.

She pours up some coffee. "Cream? I can't remember."

"Just a little is fine. Thanks. Can't take it black like I used to."

Di, Jo, Catherine and Hetch stand around the kitchen drinking their coffee and talking about life's small details, catching him up on the boys and school, etc., etc. Wouldn't want to be rude. Make your guests feel at home, Bibba had said. Offer food and drink and ask after their mamas and such. He says he is sorry to hear about Bibba.

Jo excuses herself to call home and Di needs a smoke and then, Catherine and Hetch are alone, the way they knew it would be as soon as he entered the house. They move to the table. The letters were waiting.

"She never liked you." Catherine says, picking at the string that held the letters together.

Hetch nodded. "I shouldn't be surprised that she hid them from you. I got *your* letter. I read it and reread it. I wore it thin in the creases, folding and unfolding it. I wrapped it in plastic to keep it dry. Fellas made fun of me, but we were always looking for something to laugh about." He says.

"I thought you never wrote back." Her voice is small.

"But I did." He winks.

"Why didn't you tell me? When I came back here that summer with the kids?"

"I wanted to. I wasn't sure at first, how you were feeling

about me. You were married. I thought maybe you'd forgotten how it had been between us. Once I realized what was really going on, it was too late. I couldn't bring it up with everything you were going through. Anyway, I figured something had happened to the letters, well, *something* meaning you never got them in the first place. Or you had and didn't want to write back. When I saw you I could feel it, you know? Our connection. Your mother wasn't too happy to see me that summer, though."

He is so familiar to her. Catherine pulls at the string. The stack slides off balance, the weight of his words falling open in front of them.

How long had it been? Twenty, twenty-five years? She was visiting her mother the last time she saw him. One of the few times she returned to Wimbee. She hadn't expected him to be in town. After Ryland was gone, Hetch came to her mother's house and helped take care of her and the kids. Was she relieved Ryland was dead? All she could feel was fear. Fear of what had been. Fear of the person she'd become, fear of what would happen next. The fear lived in her. She was no longer separate from it, an emotion that came and went. It *was* her. It consumed her. And she turned off the lights, shut it all down. For six months, she was not there. She was somewhere hiding in the dark. The only reason she knew it had been six months was because that's what they told her. It could have been a blink of an eye, a roll of thunder, a sudden loss of electricity and then the lights were back on.

She still wasn't sure all that Bibba, Di, and Hetch had taken care of while her mind was hiding. When she waked, her kids were taller, older. Someone had fed them, bathed them, provided for them. It was a terrifying experience to wake up and find things so different. Was it really true? Had all of this time passed? Where had she been?

Jo was happy to see some light in her mother's eyes and

then she was angry and back and forth. Catherine didn't blame her. She took Jo's anger and swallowed it. It felt right to take it. David wasn't the baby she remembered. He was indifferent to his mother's coming around. She called his name and he would turn to her and then turn away as if she weren't there, as if he'd heard something far away calling to him. Then she realized who had kept her babies alive and it was they and her children who had not let her slip away. They had held on to her when she couldn't even hold a spoon to her own mouth. Somewhere in her brain she knew she needed to come back, that she was missing them, missing time, and that they needed her as much as she needed them. It was so hard to come back. It would have been easier to stay away.

She's not sure what triggered her return. She was suddenly there again and it hadn't felt like a choice. More like a push, a shove out of the shadows back into life, naked and reeling and stepping out of the forest and into the clearing. The sun was shining, blindingly shining, her eyes swimming in tears. Her brain struggled to catch up. Another six months passed before she could handle the day to day. Conversations, loud noises, showers, the dishes, the laundry, the bills, the job search, and the guilt.

She sent Hetch away. She promised him that she was incapable of loving him, that he should go away from her, forget her. I am not who you think I am. I am not the woman you want to love. My body, my mind, my soul have separated. I am not whole. I am frayed and worn and stretched thin and your love is so full and heavy and I cannot hold it. And she was right. Love is a lot to carry. The love for her children sustained her. It made her get up in the morning. But the kind of love Hetch had for her was the kind she couldn't return. Not then. Because he was Hetch, *is* Hetch, has always been Hetch, he understood. Told her he would go away and let her mend. Because that was love. It was reminiscent of another time. Her telling him to go, him wanting nothing more than to stay. Why did she always have to push? Wasn't she trying to do what was right? For once. She thanked him and felt forever in his debt and watched him go while Jo yelled at her asking her why, why was she doing this, why was she making him go. She replayed the words he'd whispered to her while her mind was in the dark: Come back to us, Cat, I love you, Cat, he's gone gone gone.

Catherine told Bibba it was time for her and the kids to leave. She had to get out. Run. The only other place she knew was Lenoir, which seemed strange at first, but she needed simple decisions. A brand new place seemed like a mountain she was in no shape to climb. She wanted to know where the grocery store was, the gas station, movie store. She tried not to make things too hard for herself and the kids. She packed their things and Di drove them back. They crossed the same bridges, went by the same trees, traveled familiar roads. Jo cried all the way.

Catherine found out later that Hetch made arrangements, sold his place and left because it was over this time. Move on. Find someone else and leave all the broken pieces behind. The next time she saw him, years later when she was visiting her mother, he had returned home. Missed the island. Missed his business. He seemed guarded, shaded by their past. She was different. Better.

How are you? Fine, and you? Good. You look nice, you're hair and all, he said. Thanks. Just trying something new. The girls at work like it. Work, he asks. Yes. Belks. The department store. Been there for a while now. Right, sounds good, he nods. And you? I thought you were...well, I don't know where, come to think of it.

* * *

"I don't even know why Jo and Di stuck around as long as they did." Catherine says, eyeing Di on the front porch.

"I'd like to think they wanted to see me." He says.

Hetch put his hands on the table, long fingers spread out. She remembers those hands. There's just something about the right man's hands. She is startled by her urge to reach out and touch him. He leans back in his chair showing the length of his arms. He takes a deep breath and relaxes himself.

"Do you want to see me?" He asks.

There it was. It was the sound of a single coin hitting the offering plate in a quiet sanctuary. The only question. The always question. It was their story: seemingly simple and open- ended. The only problem was that it wasn't really one question. It was a ball of questions, wrapped and tangled around one another going this way and that.

Do I want to see you? Do I, the woman who didn't choose you time and time and over and over, the woman who was wrecked and crushed, whose soul was so depleted it wasn't even a whisper of what it was when you first loved her. Want? To want dismisses the necessity, it implies a momentary fix, a satiation, when what I am is in need. I need. I have always needed. To see you? Yes Yes. To see you, to touch you, to hold you. You, the man who has always held my heart gently but firmly, never letting me go, with such hope that I would turn to you, to come away with you. You saved me and saved me and save me now. But I cannot ask you to love me.

"You know I always enjoy seeing you, Hetch."

"I love you, Cat." His eyes are soft. The scruff on his face is gray. He is gray in all the right places.

Can she stand it? She rubs her thumb up and down the curve of the cup handle. This man sitting in front of her had, for so long, been a clear presence, almost a hallucination. She had imagined him sitting next to her at home, in the car, out on a walk, in her bed. She'd dreamed of his smile that always showed in his eyes. She'd reached for his hand not knowing what they looked like with age, but imagined them to be much the same and watched the vision of him soften and then hover like fog, disappearing with her breath. And now his presence was real, not conjured like some child's fanciful dream. He was a man with a heartbeat and air in his lungs and she could say with confidence that she hadn't made him up. She could smell his earthiness, his sawdust and pine. He did exist. He had loved her. And says he still does. How can that be? How can life be filled with such extremes?

He picks up a letter. "Open it, Cat. Any one of them. Doesn't matter. They all say the same thing. I was begging you. My heart was in your hands. I was wanting you and needing you, especially then because there were so few beautiful things for me to think on. Except for you. You were, are, my beautiful."

"I didn't know."

"Yes, you did. I've never felt any other kind of way and you know that."

"You shouldn't forgive me."

"But I do."

"Say it again." She says.

"I love you, Cat."

"I didn't do right by you. I tried to make you see. You didn't have to do all you did. I was never able...never deserved anything from you. How could you possibly..."

"I love you."

She shakes her head. "It wouldn't be right. How old are we? There's not enough time."

He leans in. "Say it. Say it, Cat."

She looks at him, her lips are pressed tightly together.

She takes a small breath. "I love you, Thomas."
He smiles. "I know."

21

Jo

Jo tugs at the fitted sheet corner. She smoothes out the wrinkles and tucks the top sheet in on the sides and then covers the bed with a quilt. She looks around the room. She straightens one of the framed flowers and wipes the dust off the top of her dresser. Her suitcase is tucked into the corner of her closet, the corner where David used to hide. Sometimes she would crawl in with him. They would sit not saying anything. Di would find them and coax them out with promises of ice cream or banana pudding. Bibba used to lie with her in this twin bed when she couldn't sleep. Their bodies pressed together, the solidness of Bibba keeping her in the present, grounding her to the earth.

The window of her room looked out on to the porch. She remembers sitting out there and sucking the juices out of boiled peanuts before breaking the shells open with her teeth, occasionally throwing a nut or two to Bogue, Bibba's dog. You rascal, she'd say and let him lick the salt off her fingers. He was a good dog. Bibba never trusted anyone who didn't like dogs. Jo remembers how Bibba used to talk to Bogue like he was a person. Yes, I am making this sandwich. I see you there. But it's not for you, she would say before throwing him a slice of turkey. He was always happy to see Jo. Didn't matter if she were gone two hours or five minutes, he would slobber and wag and jump and bark just because she walked into the room. He would wait for her after school to share her snack with her on the porch. Jo loved him for that. His love was so dependable. She smiles thinking of the way he would groan as he settled down for the night, his body tightly curled with his tail tucked in under his nose. She misses seeing him squint in the early morning sunshine, yawning and stretching, just happy to be. He was a great comfort to her and when he died of old dog age, she felt a hollowness and also guilt because she knew she hadn't felt the same despair when her father was buried.

What had she felt when Daddy died? Afraid. She had felt afraid, which didn't make a whole lot of sense. The monster was gone, wasn't he? But when the monster is invisible, isn't he even more frightening? Yes. It's like in the movies: hearing footsteps getting closer; breath down the back of your neck in the darkness is a lot scarier than the three-eyed monster chasing you down the street in broad daylight.

The grandmother she'd never met showed up a few weeks after her father's death while Jo was playing in the front yard with Bogue. She walked up the gravel driveway taking slow and careful steps. Bogue growled. Jo told him to quiet and he whined and sat down.

The woman stopped and looked at Jo. "I'm Sally Evans." She was a wiry woman with deep set eyes and paper-like skin. She reminded Jo of a desert bush; she looked wind-blown and parched, but somehow surviving. She wore a light-colored dress that fell over her body. Jo stared at her blue and purple veined ankles. She carried a small black pocket-book.

"You're Ryland's daughter." Her voice was like two pieces of sandpaper rubbing together.

Jo was uneasy. "Yes, ma'am. I am. Can I help you?"

"Josephine, isn't it?"

"Yes."

"He's dead, aint he?"

"Yes. Did you need something? Do you want to talk to Bibba?"

"No, child. I just came to check. Bull's dead, too, couple of years back. So, it's done now." The old woman turned and went back the way she came.

Jo tried to picture her father as a child. What was he like as a baby, all wrapped up in a blanket, innocent and pink like David was? She imagined being something small and insignificant, something he carried with him that he wouldn't care to hit or scream at or throw away. Maybe his comb, or wallet. A lucky penny. What would it be like to be in his hands and for him to use her with ease, for him to hold her without squeezing so hard it made her eyes water? He wouldn't have to care that much about her, like say, the rubber band he kept on his wrist in case he needed it. Or the bandana he kept stuffed in his back pocket in case he started to sweat. How would that feel? To be near him and not afraid? To be against his skin, gently, casually, to feel the hairs on his arm brush against her or to be tied around him, so close and personal. For him to notice her, but not see her as an opportunity to terrorize or humiliate, just as something that's there, that exists giving her the chance to see him as simply a man.

He was everywhere all the time. She saw him in the trucks on the road that looked like the one he used to drive. He was the man walking down the street with the baseball cap, hands in his pockets. He was in her bathroom before she turned on the light. She saw him in David's face, so much so these days that it was difficult to look at him. It wasn't just David's features. It was the way he tilted his head forward, eyes looking up at her. It was the sound of his angry breathing and the way he would pick at his nails. She was afraid of his control over her.

When they were kids it was hard to look away from David, to ignore him. There was something enticing and beautiful about his intensity. It was like he knew the secrets she'd protected, nestled behind her ribcage, deep, dark, and vibrating with the beating of her heart. He saw through it all and triggered the vacuum of her madness.

The last time she visited him, he had lashed out at her, growling and spitting in her face. He reached for her and managed to grab her wrist because she hadn't moved. There was something in her that wanted to connect. She wanted to help the one other person who knew what it was like to be a child in their family. He knew. A nurse moved quickly and freed Jo's arm, while another nurse restrained him and tried to calm him down. It wasn't working. Jo backed away from him. The nurses injected him with a medication. Jo rubbed her wrist, trying to wipe him away. It wasn't right. He was a reminder. She shouldn't want to be near him. She watched the medication work through his body. He clammed up, his breathing wet in his throat. She watched as his focus drained, just eyes looking out into the nothing. They moved him to a wheelchair and took him away.

Before she left, his doctor showed her David's latest drawings. She held the bound artist notebook and recognized it as one she brought him some other time before. She flipped it open and turned the pages slowly, the doctor's voice fading out, becoming softer until it was the sound of a moth fluttering by her ear. She saw her face. In pen and pencil, drawn with heavy lines and squared off shapes. She turned the page. She saw her head above water, her eyes wide and frantic. Her mother was there, too, on her own page. He'd written over her face and filled the page with writing that was so small she could hardly read it. She wasn't sure she wanted to, anyway. She knew it was a synthesis of poetry, voices, lines from books he'd read. The first time she'd seen his writing like this, she imagined a symphony, layers on layers of musical instruments playing different notes, the sounds individual, but fusing in an attempt to connect. What was it he was trying to say? She closed the notebook and felt an overwhelming sadness.

What had she said? What set him off like that? Mama wanted to know what she'd done.

Did you provoke him? You know he doesn't like it when you talk too loud or too much. Sometimes I think you make him feel like you're more important, with your job and your family. He doesn't have those things. It makes him feel bad about himself, Jo. Can't you just talk about the weather or sports? He likes to talk about sports.

Yes, Mama.

Jo throws the pillows onto the bed, their fresh from the linen closet smell all around her. She calls Will.

"Hey." He picks up on the first ring.

"Wow. You're never going to guess who showed up." She says sitting on the bed.

"Oh, let me see. Hetch, I bet."

"How'd you know?"

"Because I'm good at these things." He says.

"I don't know why I didn't see that coming. He does live here."

"I don't know. Maybe you did see it coming. And hoped it would happen."

* * *

When her mother brought Jo and David back to Lenoir, after everything that happened, it was hard for Jo to imagine herself as an adult, growing up, getting a job, much less going to college. She could only focus on the day ahead of her. I'm going to eat this muffin for breakfast. I will get through school today. I will make sure David has showered and brushed his teeth before bed. There were months after her return that, looking back now, seemed like one long day. The longest day. They didn't return to their old house. Her mother rented one side of a two- bedroom duplex not far from school. Di stayed with them, slept on the couch. Jo returned to her old school. Kids gawked and whispered. When asked, she said she'd been visiting her grandmother during the summer, had decided to live there because who wouldn't want to live at the beach, but her mother decided they needed to move back to stupid Lenoir. Her mother hadn't even asked what she'd wanted, she'd say, because if it had been up to her, she would have never left. Teachers smiled and patted her hand and welcomed her home. She missed Lisa. Jo felt like she was floating underwater in a pond, maybe, no current; the water was still and clouded with small bits of dirt and bark and parts of insects. That's what she imagined, anyway. It was so hard to see through. She didn't try to swim. Floating was easier, staying under.

And then Will showed up.

Jo was taking the trash out to the street. It was evening and she'd spent her time after school sitting on the floor of her room waiting for her mother to come home from work. She rubbed her hand over a line inside the crease of her elbow. It was scabbed over. She picked at the small bumps that looked like morse code and it started to bleed again. She licked her finger and wiped it away. David sat in front of the TV Her mother did come home. Jo felt like she could move, then, get up and boil some water for a pot of rice, just like Bibba had showed her. Fifteen minute boil, no more—no less and then drain.

After supper, she was helping to clean up. The sky was turning from a purple-gray to a deep blue and the street light buzzed on as she stepped outside. She twisted the doorknob to make sure she wouldn't lock herself out and scanned the yard and street before closing the door. Will was riding a bicycle back and forth in front of the house. He wasn't even holding the handlebars. He needed a haircut.

"Hey." He said.

Jo's nose wrinkled. She looked around.

"I said, Hey."

"Yeah. I heard you."

Moths started flying up and hitting the street lamp.

"Well, why'd you not say it back?"

"Cause."

"Cause what?"

"I don't know. Didn't feel like it."

"Oh."

They stared at each other. Jo sighed. "What are you doing out here, anyway?"

"Just riding around."

"Shouldn't you be at home now?"

"Maybe, I mean, I don't know. I don't live far."

"Fine."

"Just bored, I guess." Will rode around in a circle.

"Yeah."

"You ever get bored?"

"Sure. Sometimes."

"Yeah, me too...you're in my class, you know."

"I know."

"Did you do the math homework?"

"Yep." Jo lied.

"Well, I gotta go. See you at school."

"See ya."

Jo watched him bike away. He was out in the dark by himself and didn't seem to care. She realized he hadn't asked her where she'd been or why she came back. She thought about how his hair hung in his eyes.

That's how it was between them, a *hello* here and there, the catch of an eye in class or at lunch. They had something in common, each of them could feel it. Jo didn't know what the thing was and she found herself wondering about him, wanting to know more, but feeling frightened by the idea of knowing someone else. They kept their distance, each silently plotting each other's whereabouts, times and dates on mental maps. They happened to run into one another at the grocery store. Just picking up something. Or at the movie rental store. Just returning this. Out by the lake. I'm just on my way home.

It wasn't until after Jo walked into the lake that they became inseparable. Somehow he'd known to ride his bike down to the lake that day. He came to visit her, held her hand while she stared out the hospital room window. He talked to her. She listened. He told her she didn't have to talk, that he understood. She didn't say anything. He said everything: His mother was slowly dying, he sometimes wished she would, he ate microwave dinners almost every night, he loved school and baseball and Led Zeppelin, his father was hardly ever home, his father doesn't know how to do laundry, his father doesn't love him, his mother will never get better, he is lonely most of the time, he will make sure his kids are happy.

The sound of his voice still settles her still.

Jo said, "What'd y'all do for supper tonight?"

"Burgers. Fries. Milkshakes. And then we sat around in our underwear and farted all over the furniture. Guy stuff."

Jo can't hold back her laughter and lies back on the bed like she's thirteen talking to her crush. The only thing missing is her finger twirling in her hair.

"Not sorry I'm missing that, to be honest." She laughs again. "Mama is in there talking to him right now. I gave her the letters. And, I didn't even peek at them! I came into the bedroom to give them some space. Di found him at the grocery store."

"Did she throw him over her shoulder like a sack of potatoes?"

"I doubt he needed much persuading." Jo yawns. "This has been the longest day. Didn't get to talk to Brian earlier. How's he doing?" She rubs her hand over the old wedding ring quilt that Bibba had made a long time ago.

"He's great. They're all in there watching a movie together. They didn't even fight over what to watch."

"Oh." She says. "So, he's happy and not sulking?"

"He seems good."

Jo feels her face flush. She is jealous. "This feels so stupid. I don't know. I just feel like if I were there he wouldn't be happy."

"Jo, I don't think that's true."

"It feels true. And we've invested a lot in therapy for me to be able to describe what I'm really feeling. You get to have him there with you and he's in a good mood and happy and I don't get to see him like that anymore. I know it sounds like an exaggeration. I feel like he's depressed, but only around me. What have I done to him?"

"I think you're being a little sensitive about this, which is okay, I'm not judging, I'm just saying I think..."

"You think I'm over-analyzing it." She sits up. "And that is judging, by the way.

"Yeah." He finally says.

Jo rolls her eyes and her throat tightens. "You think I'm

being a clingy mother."

"No, that's not at all what I said. Please don't get defensive."

Defensive. Jo almost hangs up. She holds her breath for a second, not sure what to say. She wants to whine like a child, wants to argue and prove she's right. Her cheeks are hot. She juts her jaw forward and throws an arm in the air as if he can see her exasperation.

She speaks in a low tone trying to control her voice, "Next, are you going to tell me to be calm? I'm not being defensive. I just think you're playing this down, like there's nothing going on. Like I'm worrying too much." Her voice is rising. She hates when she sounds shrill, like she's lost control, an overly-emotional woman, but she can't hold back. She wishes she could be the one to say 'I think *you* need to calm down' because she knew that was the power move. And she also knew, from therapy, that that was *de*structive instead of *con*structive. There was something about showing your emotions that held truth. Only, there are high-stakes in being so vulnerable. The composed person, the one who is always under control is the one that has more at stake, at least she tells herself. With Jo, Will always knows where she stands.

"Well, you know what? This is how kids get into trouble. Parents don't see the warning signs. Maybe you're not worrying enough."

"I don't think that's fair." His voice is firm.

"Life isn't fair," She says. So now she's sarcastic.

Jo waits for him to say something.

"Really, Jo? Now you're being childish. I think maybe we should just talk tomorrow. You've got a lot on your mind right now. You just left a job you've worked really hard at for a long time, you're trying to say 'goodbye' to your grandmother, you've been cooped up with your mother and aunt..."

"Fine. I guess that was childish, but stop being my psychiatrist and just be my husband...I should go anyway. Tell the boys I love them." They say the right things to each other to keep it all intact, but their voices are cold.

Jo throws the phone on the bed. "Goddammit." She didn't handle that well and will be apologizing in the morning. He better apologize, too, though.

22

Diana

Di didn't want to pry. She could hear Jo on the phone, but the girl was loud and had her window open. Not much Di could do. Not sure where else she could go. Catherine and Hetch needed their privacy, too. Hell, they need a lot more than that. She lit a cigarette and stared at the moon over the row of houses across the street.

The best of sisters. Catherine and Di were always close. Mama made sure they were together all the time. They were close enough in age to have the same friends, hang out in the same groups. They grew up knowing what it meant to be loyal. They were two rivers born from the same mountain who, after their father died, as they flowed through the valley of death, converged into one. And so when Catherine got married it seemed like a slap in the face. She's leaving. Going away. What the hell am I supposed to do now? She remembers feeling separated, like having a right hand without the left. Yes, she'd followed them to Lenoir. Mama wanted her to and she wanted to, she'd guessed. She could see Ryland as the pig he was and wanted so badly for Catherine to see it, too. She should have said something. She couldn't. Honesty was too risky. She knew Catherine wouldn't listen and might abandon her completely. No. Not ever that. She waited for Catherine to push through this delusion, for the dam to break, for her to see with clearer, fresher eyes. But when Catherine got pregnant with Jo, Di lost hope that Catherine would get away. What else was there for Di except to stay and wait? She found her job at the storage business and met Billy.

Horrible dresser. The first time she met him, he was wearing a t-shirt he'd found at a thrift store. She was fine with second-hand clothes, just not ones that advertised the local funeral home. One of his favorite shirts had a silhouette of a man running and the words *Miles For Smiles* on it. He'd pat his potbelly and laugh. Not that she was hooked on fashion . They didn't make the man as far as she was concerned. What did make a man was his heart. She'd seen enough not to risk losing herself over the man with money who had no personality, the man who'd rather she not sit beside him but behind him. No, she didn't want those guys. She'd chew them up and spit them out. Even though she'd loved her daddy and was willing to look past his mistakes, and because he'd broken her heart, too, she wasn't looking for him in a man. The thing was, she knew her mother wasn't innocent and as hard as it was to admit, even a man with a good heart can do bad things. No, she was looking for her own kind of man, a man like Billy.

Billy was different. Hawaiian shirts and jean shorts, ball caps that covered his balding head. He better not want kids, better not be paying alimony. I don't want any of that baggage, she told him. A beer every weekend's okay, but I don't want a drinker. I need my own money and my own car.

Billy said okay to all. She watched his green eyes, waited for them to betray him, wanted to see the green turn to yellow, his irises closing in on themselves turning into long vertical slits. She stood behind the storage room door in the office and listened to him talk to customers, listened for his voice to harden, deepen, for him to threaten or yell or hiss, especially when he was talking to people who hadn't paid for their unit. He'd rub his hand back and forth over his head while he thought over a problem, his big meaty hand with callouses built up over the years working as a mover, a hauler of people's things. She waited for his hands to ball into fists, to come crashing down with a WHAM like someone has slammed a heavy screen door. She expected him to slide silently behind her, to wrap himself around her, squeeze the life out of her. But then, she realized who he truly was.

He was a man who, for a long time, was lonely. He'd tried not to be. Tried to be social, but never quite found his footing in the world. He was special in a way that only she could see. He was kind. He asked her if she knew Jesus because that was his only requirement. She can have all the problems in the world as long as she's willing to share his heart with The Lord. She said she hadn't met him personally (that she knows of), but she's a Christian, if that's what he means. He accepted this on account of her large bosom.

Surprisingly, to some, Di had not turned out to be a tramp.

They planned on marrying. Getting a dog. Buying a house. She wanted to take a cruise, not sure where to yet, but they had time to figure it out. The summer she drove Catherine and the kids to Bibba's, the summer Ryland showed up to get them, that summer, Di was only twenty-seven. Billy was thirty-five. He understood what she was doing and why. Jo used to come into the office sometimes and Billy would give her a piece of peppermint candy. He always had peppermints. Sweet kid, he would say. Di would say, yeah, she's just like her Mama and would smile. He would put an arm around Di's shoulder and they'd watch Jo skip across the parking lot. Then, they'd sit together and go through the latest newspaper advertisement to send to the paper. They would walk the grounds together checking the locks on the units. She would sweep the front office floor and he'd fix the latest paper jam in the printer. They kept things simple and enjoyed their little piece of the world together.

So, when he called to say that Ryland had come by asking questions, Di got to worrying.

Billy, honey, watch out for Ryland, honey. You know there's no reasoning with him. Don't go to talking to him about Jesus and how he can be saved, now, honey, just listen, don't do that. He won't hear you. All right, doll, he says. I won't, he says. I just like to help when I can, he says. I know, baby, she says, I know. You're a good man with a good heart.

That very summer, in September, when Di and Catherine heard the truck's engine, their heads jerked up like deer hearing the slightest sound in the woods. Shit, says Di, and Catherine says, No no no, Di! Don't do anything. We need to hide. Hide! She is frantic. Where's Bibba, asks Di picking up the phone, and then they realize she is out untangling the garden hose in the yard. And then there she is, holding a shovel on her shoulder, body centered, waiting. Catherine is on the phone when Di sees her mother. Oh, hell no, says Di and goes out to stand next to her mama. He is out of the truck just laughing and laughing at the sight of these two women. As if you bitches even think you can take me, he says. We've called the cops, says Di, which is true. Catherine has also called the school and they are praying, Please, God, keep Jo safe at school. Di looks at Ryland and tries to say calm things to him. Let's talk about this, she says. You're not a bad man, she lies. I know you want to do right, she says. He smiles and says Billy was a goddamned liar with his Jesus crap. Di hears

Ryland say *was* and it's in this moment that she knows her heart is dead. Ryland points his finger at her and fires an imaginary gun. Di can't breathe. She stumbles back against the porch railing. She doesn't notice the sirens.

The cops come. Then Catherine is outside with her suitcase because she already knows how this is going to go. Everyone else seems less sure. Catherine, you can't do this! Yells Di. These damn cops, with their old-boy bullshit. They don't know him. They do know him, should know him. They see him all the time in other houses hitting and cussing and killing other women just like Catherine. They know this is real. Get back on the porch, ladies, they say to Bibba and Di. They tell Catherine to be calm. Don't go, please, says Di who is now holding David because this baby has come out of the house instead of staying inside where she'd left him. Bye Bye, sweet boy, says Catherine and David is crying. Ryland grabs Catherine and tells her not without his boy, they aren't leaving without the boy. That's when Di sees the gun in Ryland's hand. He's pressing it on Catherine's head forcing her to bend her neck. She says, Please, just let him be. You don't want him. Just let him stay here. And Di's brain is on fire. What is she supposed to do? Ryland yanks Catherine's arm and tells Di to bring David down and whispers something in Catherine's ear. Now, now, says the cops. God damn you! Di yells. Di, bring David down the stairs, Catherine says, but Di won't. The cops are telling Ryland to let her go, but it's not right. You Goddamned men! All of you! Di is crying and Bibba is shaking with fury, tears streaming down her face and Catherine is crying and these women, who all look so much alike, are all crying the same tears. And there is Hetch running up the driveway and then Jo. My God, there is Jo.

After Ryland jumped and Catherine and Jo and David were taken, after the bridge, and the rest, while the sky was dark gray and the rain sounded like marbles hitting the roof of the patrol car, she and Bibba were taken down to the police station. A detective from Lenoir was there. Miller was his name. She'll never forget. She remembers what he told her. She believed him, knew that it was true. She screamed at him, You're wrong! It's not Billy! But he was not wrong. It was her Billy. Di dropped to the floor.

At night, in the quiet, she is alone and doesn't want to sleep. Tell me again, about the plan, she says to Billy. She is lying in the crook of his arm. He is with her and his eyes are bright. Oh, you know, he says, the start of a smile on his face. We save up, get us a place, put in some new technology around here in the office, computers and stuff. Some cameras, maybe. She smiles at his small dreams. Then she feels a change, a swirl of direction and then she is there in Lenoir. She imagines she is at the office. She doesn't want to open the door, but she does. She sees his body on the floor. One hole in his head and one hole in his heart. And she knows he is with Jesus and that should make her feel better because she knows that's what he would want, but it doesn't. It hurts, it just hurts. All she can think is it doesn't look like this in the movies.

She hears the porch door close and opens her eyes.

Bibba

December 18, 2014

Oh, Jo. That damn dog. I am sitting her crying big fat tears because it is Bogue's birthday. I feel like I owe him so much more than a hole in the ground and a rock as a marker. Do you remember how he used to chase the seagulls? He would curl up next to you on your bed. He always knew when you were having a hard night going to sleep. He was always protecting you.

You know, I got him shortly after the girls left the house for Lenoir. The house was just so quiet. He was a terrible puppy. Chewed things, peed everywhere. Connie would have thrown him out in the yard. But not me. I saw him and he saw me. I set some boundaries and with time, he grew into the dog you knew. He could put on a good show, but never had a mean bone in his body.

It had been a long time since I'd had to really care for anyone. Must have been eight or nine years since Connie died.

Connie, being a doctor himself, saw the signs of cancer. Why, then, would he choose to ignore them for so long? I'll tell you why: penance. It wasn't until Nadine's engagement party that I knew the real reason he married me. Well, maybe he did still love me, but that wasn't it. He married me out of guilt. Had he walked into the church that day a few minutes sooner, would he have been able to stop it? Why did he let that man walk by and out of the church? Let that man laugh in his face? Accept that an investigation or follow-thru of any kind would be too much for me? He let them hush it up.

Because he was weak.

I know that sounds harsh and even cruel. It hits right at the center of a man's ego to say such a thing. But it was the truth. His fragility was a wound that wouldn't heal. Yes, we had children, but mostly he couldn't bring himself to touch me. That does something to a woman. You might wonder how a woman with my history could want to be in a room alone with a man. That implies that a woman raped is a woman ruined. And that's just not so. True, she is changed, but there is nothing that says she can't be whole again. Men are made out to be the only ones that are interested in sex, but there's nothing wrong with women enjoying it, too, even those of us who survived such violence.

Now don't balk, Jo. I know I'm old and look like a dried apricot, but I haven't always been this way. It's about intimacy and the feeling of being wanted. A woman's body is a wonderful thing. Can do so many things. And after the children are born and have used a woman's body for living, she should be able to get her body back. To enjoy it with someone. Connie just couldn't. It was just as well. When I looked in the mirror, I could see what he saw. I was a walking, breathing, blood-pumping-through-my-veins punch in the gut. I was his truth, the proof of the man he wasn't. So, he slept with other women.

Nurses from his office, friends of friends of friends. I cared in the beginning. I felt so foolish. People knew before I did. It was embarrassing. The pity caught in their throats like toast crumbs making them cough and excuse themselves not wanting to be around me. I got mad, delusional almost. Even tried to run one woman off the road before I came to my senses. And then I just stopped. I stopped asking him questions, stopped caring where or with whom he was.

The girls didn't understand. Children never do and we shouldn't ask them to. They felt the saturated silence between us. Catherine took it especially hard, probably because she was the older one. She was angry. Di was just heartbroken for all of us. They know of at least one of the affairs. I found them in the hallway listening during one of our arguments and then had to explain while tears ran down their faces, arms around each other, holding on as if the other was her single piece of drift-wood floating in a wide open sea. It hurt them so. But the truth does that sometimes.

When he got sick, it was hard for him. I kept him here in

193

the house for as long as I could. I cared for him myself. It was a level of intimacy that we hadn't shared in quite some time. I had to feed him, bathe him, help him to the bathroom. It was difficult for him. I loved him through all of it, and at times, in spite of what he wanted. It would have been easier for him if I'd called him a coward or blamed him. But I honestly don't know that he could have changed things. What was done, was done. Could he have stopped the rape? Saved me from the humiliation of seeing Henry at the engagement party? Yes. He froze in the church those many years ago, undecided, unsure of what to do. That one moment of inaction became the noose around his neck. It wasn't the cancer that killed him, it was the guilt.

Divorce was not common those days and I'm not sure that's what I would have wanted. I was too afraid of being on my own, which at this age, sounds ridiculous to me. Women didn't talk openly about marital problems-not like they do now (and too openly, I might add). It felt like I was stranded. I was the only one. Everyone else appeared to have happy marriages and children and families without struggle. There is far too much sharing of personal problems these days. Not everyone has to know everything. But perhaps talking more openly with Catherine and Di would have healed some things. Sometimes it's hard to know what's right, especially as a parent, especially when you're heartbroken.

But enough about that. Because today is about Bogue, so I am going out to get some cake.

23

Catherine

Catherine looks at Hetch standing on the porch, the sun setting, enhancing his profile, and realized what an incredible turn life can take.

She'd imagined him sitting at her table in the morning sun. The two of them having some coffee, maybe some eggs. He would tease her about burnt bacon or sausage, tell her how the neighbors repaired their gutters wrong, and she would remind him to set out the hose on a slow trickle to water the rose bush because it needed a good, long soak. He would scan the obituaries and remark on someone he knew. She would read the front page first, passing it to him when she finished. They would do the crossword and he would draw his own squares to make his words fit. She would laugh and push his hand away. Neither of them would look at the dark corner of the room, choosing instead to sit together in the light. Is it possible to have that kind of happiness? She's never dared to pray for it for herself, only for her children.

Every time Catherine looks at Jo, she sees fear in her daughter's face. Can't mistake it for sadness or anger or pity or guilt. Sadness is blue, anger is red, pity is baby pink, and guilt is a sickly yellow. Catherine has always imagined fear to be purple. Grape jelly jars smashed on the floor, backs covered in bruises, circles around sleepless eyes, broken joints, the color she would always see right before she felt herself drifting into the black.

Jo has always worn purple.

Catherine wasn't surprised by everyone's reaction to her engagement announcement. Catherine was a lucky girl. Catherine would get whatever she wanted now that Ryland had chosen her. Lots of single girls crying in their pillows wishing they'd caught his eye. How'd she managed that, they'd asked. What's so great about her? The lucky one. He was wild and fearless. He had dark hair and deep brown eyes that, at first, she thought were filled with mischief, but learned later was malice. Who was the lucky one, really?

Bibba was different.

He comes from spoiled roots, she'd said. You won't be happy. You're not thinking this through, she'd said. You were right, Bibba, Catherine thinks. Just like always. But here's the kicker: I did it on purpose. Married him knowing he would be unfaithful, knowing he would lie, break my heart, look at me with disgust. Well, not specifically those things, I couldn't have imagined what he turned out to be, but I knew he wasn't good for me. I went with him anyway. I don't know why. No, that's not true. I do know why. I did it because I was angry and heartbroken. I did it because no one wanted me to. I'd always done everything right, been a good girl, modest, smart, well-mannered. Before, I'd wanted to please you, Bibba. Once I met, Ryland, I just wanted to run. I did it because everyone else wanted him and he chose me. Just for a moment, he chose me. And that did something to me. Made me feel something I needed to feel. I existed. I mistook flattery and lust for love. And once I had that feeling, it was hard to let it go. I was such a child. I just kept thinking that if I did this a certain way or that a certain way, that he would choose me again and that feeling would come back. He had a hold on a part of me. It didn't feel like love the way it had with Hetch, but I told myself that of course it wouldn't be the same. They were two different men. Does love look different depending on the man? Over time, it was harder and harder for me to do things right. I'm not sure that we ever loved each other, but I wanted to make it work. I didn't want you to be right, Bibba. I didn't want to fail. And I look around now and see all the pain that I caused, for what? So that I could prove myself to you?

24

Jo

Jo pulls open a bag of corn chips and looks through the screen door happy to see Hetch hasn't left yet. He is sipping something from a mug, leaning on the railing. Di is smoking, sitting in the rocking chair, ashing into a soda can. Catherine steps over and stands beside Hetch. He puts his arm around her shoulders.

"Where are we going to put her?" Di asks.

"Put who?" says Catherine.

"Bibba, you knucklehead. We're supposed to be spreading her ashes."

"What would she have wanted? Maybe the open sea?" Hetch motions toward the beach.

"No." Both women say together. They smile at each other and for a moment they are young again, giggling at each other over something some boy has said.

Jo comes out on the porch. "I think we ought to leave her in the urn."

"What and just put her up on the mantel to stare at us?" Di takes a drag and blows it over her shoulder. "Here, hand me some of those."

Jo gives over the bag of chips. "Nope. Let's bury the urn. With her in it. Right next to Bogue." They all look into the yard. There was a rock underneath a forsythia bush, its branches dark and flowerless until spring.

"She loved spring time, loved watching the forsythia come to life, yellow and cheery. I think it reminded her of that old dog. And I think she would want to be beside him."

Everyone was quiet. The night-time breeze was picking up. The sea air was almost sticky.

Catherine walks down the stairs. "There is so much death in this yard already." She turns to look at them. "Maybe we shouldn't keep this house. Think about it, Di. Jo. You asked me

before about this house and what it meant to come back here, how it felt. Think about what's happened here."

"Like we could ever forget, Mama." Jo snips.

"Goddammit, Jo! Stop making me pay for this. Every damn day, I look at myself and I am ashamed." Catherine pauses, her breathing rapid. "I am ashamed at who I was and what I let happen and how I haven't had the strength to make up for it. You know what? I'm angry, too! I am so filled with anger that for a long time I thought that that was all I was ever going to feel, for the rest of my life. It's like being tarred and feathered. It coats my skin. I carry that anger with me everywhere."

Mama's hands are two tiny fists shaking in front of her chest. She looks like she will finally punch back. Her voice quiets to a whisper. "And I had to work hard to want to come back, to convince myself that I could be useful, that I deserved to be your mother. So you shut your mouth. I'm sorry I couldn't show you how much I cared in the way that you needed me to, but don't you talk to me like I don't know what happened. Parts of me have been dying all along the way: the violence, and hate, and fear; the death, our blood on everything, David locked away, you—almost drowning yourself because you couldn't take it anymore. I'm not whole! I am pieces and parts of what I was meant to be. And I'm sorry if that's not enough for you."

Jo studies the boards under her feet. She is astonished at Mama's outburst and as much as she would like to forgive and forget, her feelings are like loud, unmannered visitors. No one wanted to invite them, but here they are. What do we do with them now? They won't leave. Oh, dear. They seem to be unpacking their bags, intending to stay. They're soiling everything. What a mess, Jo thinks.

She looks at the wooden post that should be pockmarked from a shotgun blast.

It is September 10, 1986. She is eight years old again:

Jo rubs her eyes and tries to swallow. She didn't think she'd ever get to sleep with the day they'd had. She kept seeing her daddy's face and his gun. She imagines his body falling over the railing of the bridge. She imagines his dead body. She shifts in her bed trying to find her way to sleep. Bogue is with her, curled up and pressed into her side. His head is up and alert. His body is stiff, feeling, listening.

Her mouth is dry. They ate pizza for supper. Hetch picked it up after leaving the police station. They pulled up the driveway escorted by a police car, not sure what to say to each other. The policeman had assured Hetch and the women that it would be fine for them to stay the night in the house. Pizza always makes me thirsty, she thinks. She slides out of bed to get a glass of water. The floor is cold. Hetch said it would be okay to come home. He said we should try to get some rest because there would be more to do in the following days. More questions from the police, funeral arrangements, and whatever came after that. She leaves her bedroom and walks into the living room, her hand on the wall to guide her in the darkness. Mama had wanted her to sleep in the bed with her and David, but David was hard to sleep with. His knobby knees pushed into her back or he swung his sleepy arms around hitting her, waking her.

No, she said, I'll be fine in my room. They all slept with their doors open.

She notices the front door pushed back against the wall, the screen door cracked, and the darkness outside like a big, wide mouth. The door sways slightly as it does when the air is sucked out of a room. It isn't until after the door moves that her senses wake up enough to see the broken window on the front door and his shape in the shadows. For a moment, she believes it is his ghost.

What's wrong, girl? He says stepping into the light of the moon. He skin looks gray and the little hair he has is matted down on his head. She is sure he is the walking dead. He shows her a knife, swaying it back and forth in front of her face.

Daddy's back. He whispers.

He lunges at her, grabs her arm and puts a hand over her mouth. Why? There are no words there. Nothing will escape. There is no need for him to be so quick, could have moved slowly, could've pushed her over with barely a touch. Her brain is not speaking to her body. Her muscles are tightened to the point of breaking. She'll feel later like she was hit by a car, muscles sore from tension. Bogue crouches low in the shadows, growling and bearing teeth.

You better calm that dog down, he says and so she tells the dog to stay. She is changed. She is no longer the person she was one minute ago, two minutes ago, before she got out of bed. She is made of glass. Her fear is deep and reaching. It fractures her soul. I will shatter and die, she thinks. He will kill us all.

There is a loud CHCK-SHHK sound down the hall. Daddy turns with her in his arms and puts the knife to her throat. From the darkness, she walks out, shotgun level.

I've been waiting for you, Bibba says.

Daddy sneers. His breath is like rotten food. Old woman. Put that thing down. How you gonna shoot me and not her? He begins backing toward the door.

Mama! That's Di yelling from behind.

Get on back, Di. Bibba says slowly.

Jo becomes as fragile as champagne flutes stacked one on top of another; her muscles fail her, then jerk to life again. She cannot control the shaking. Is the entire house shaking down through ground?. She watches Bibba and tries not to get her throat cut. Jo's chest rises and falls too quickly. She fears she will pass out and he will cut her throat. Oh, the things he can do to her, to Mama, to them all.

A dark mass moves down the hall. Jo hears a small voice Take me. Take me Take me. Mama walks in repeating the words and holding her arms out to him. She is in her nightgown. Di's screams are high and wailing,

No! Catherine, come back here! Bogue is up and barking. Di catches Mama by the arm before she can go any farther. Bibba is barefoot. She is stepping carefully, matching Daddy's distance as he goes backward through the screen door. Jo won't realize until later that she has walked over broken glass on the door mat. He smells the same like beer and sweat, like mud and rusty water.

You ain't gonna do nothin' Daddy spits. Just like always. He cackles. You think people don't know? Don't know about all those times your husband stepped out on you? And then you were left wiping his ass, feeding him through a tube while he died in your cold bed. My daddy told me about you. A whore. I bet you liked it. That man's hands all over you in the church. He snarls. You ain't got the guts.

They are out on the porch now. Bibba staring at the knife on Jo's neck. Bibba holding her arm steady. Jo, girl. Look at me, Jo. But Jo can't focus. All she can see is her mother. All she wants is to go to her mother.

Don't you talk to her! He is yelling again.

Bibba says, JO, louder than they were all expecting. Jo feels Daddy's hand jerk. The blade cuts into her skin. Her nose is running and she can feel his hands slipping around with sweat. Mama is behind Bibba begging him and Di is losing control, unable to keep Mama from running forward. Jo looks at Bibba. What should she do? Has Bibba always been this strong? Daddy makes a growling sound and pushes the knife harder against Jo's throat and Jo is sure she will die.

Bibba's breathing is easy. Are you a lady, Jo?

What? Daddy cocks his head. Strange thing to say. He is breathing hard on her shoulder. His focus on the knife slackens. The knife eases away from Jo's throat. Jo's eyes flicker with life. He doesn't understand. He has let his guard down, if only for a second. Is she a lady? Or is she the girl on the playground that had the courage to slap that boy? She slows her breathing. She will trust Bibba.

No ma'am. I am not, she says. Bibba whistles. Bogue is up the steps in a flash. Jo elbows her father as hard as she can at the same time that Bogue is sinking his teeth into his calf. Jo feels the knife fall away from her skin. She drops away to the side. Bogue Bogue! Daddy swings down with his knife. Bibba fires a shot above Daddy's head. He falls to the floor and out the door onto the porch. Bogue runs. Bibba reloads, quick and smooth.

Daddy yelling, spitting, holding his hands over his head. You crazy bitch! Bibba is still pointing the gun at him. She gets closer. He crawls away from her.

I missed on purpose, she says. He crawls down the stairs yelling for her to stop STOP. She doesn't. She is standing over him now. Okay, Okay, he is saying. He is on his back in the mud, his hands in front of his face. Please Please! She looks down at him.

They just graze you with that bullet? Your arm maybe? Pretty far jump off the bridge. Couldn't fool me, though. You'd know your way around those marshes even if you were blind. Her voice is calm and measured. She walks around his body never letting the barrel drop. What about, Billy, huh? Is he dead?

God, please, he says.

She pushes the barrel into his cheek. He looks like a rabid animal. What about pointing a gun at my girl's head? You son-of- a-bitch! She eases up the barrel. Believe it or not, I'm a forgiving woman. He lowers his hands a bit.

Oh, Jesus, thank you, God, he mutters spit dripping out of the side of his mouth.

She raises the gun again. But you. You have no soul and you will rot, by God, you will rot for what you've done.

Jo hears sirens. Do it, Bibba. You've got to do it now.

Mama is out on the porch, swaying, unsteady on her feet.

David is watching from the kitchen.

Di is pushing Jo back. Get inside, she is saying firmly.

No! I won't! I have to see! I have to know what's real! Jo is yelling, tearing at Di's arms. She runs over to stand beside Mama.

Bibba says, Get up. He is in a ball covering his face. She says it again, kicking his side. He is wary and whimpering as he stands. She backs up toward the porch, putting space between them.

No. Bibba! You have to do it! Jo yells.

The sirens are close.

Mama cries out. She is trembling. Di puts her hand on Mama's shoulder.

Never going back.

Bibba pulls the trigger.

Mama is screaming. Jo falls to her knees. She is sobbing. She sees blue and red flashes. Jo reaches for David who is standing beside her, his eyes locked on their father's body. Bibba puts down the gun and raises her arms all the while humming a song to herself.

Jo looks at her sixty year old mother standing in the spot where his body lay, his blood soaking into the mud, mixing with the water and earth. It could still be there under layers of dirt and ground up shells and bones, under the grass, or perhaps it was washed away or diluted and turned into vapor, which rose into the clouds to rain down on them again.

"Mama, if we keep this place or not. Nothing's going to change." She pauses, looks out at the forsythia. "The house is just a house. It's just a place. So, I'll leave it up to you."

Jo goes inside.

25

Diana

The sun is coming up. Di is still in her clothes from the day before. She hears voices in the kitchen. Hetch and Catherine. You MINX, she whispers, picturing Catherine and Hetch romantically entwined. OH. MY. GOD. She sits back and covers her mouth. It's an incredible thing to realize someone you love, who has been waiting and hurting for so long, has reached out and taken hold of happiness. However fleeting it may be, whatever comes, her sister will know the weight of a full heart.

Di flings open her door. "Well, well." She says, a big smile on her face. She points at Hetch, "And where did YOU sleep last night?"

"She loves me, Di." he says.

"For God's sakes, I know that, Hetch. Hell, the whole world knows that. Those frigging pelicans out there know that. Y'all love each other. The great love of the century and all that."

Catherine smiles and shakes her head. "Hush, Di."

Di looks at the two of them and wishes she were sitting

with Billy. She can hear him even now: You and me and Jesus makes three, he'd say. Every once in a while she lets herself imagine what life could have been. He'd get the paper and water the plants. She would make the coffee. They would eat pancakes together. Her heart pounds hard three times in her chest. She reaches out for a chair, steady steady, while not alarming anyone.

"Looks like there's hope for y'all yet." She smiles.

Catherine motions toward the counter. "There's pancakes, if you want some."

"No, thanks. Listen, I think I know what I'd like to do."

Catherine looks up at Di, "Oh? What do you mean?"

Di pulls out the chair and sits. "Let's sell."

"Oh, Di, come on. You don't think we ought to do that."

"Why not?"

"Well, because. It's Bibba's house, our house. Seems wrong for it not to stay with us."

Di sighs and looks around. "Jo's right. It's just a place. The only reason we've held on to it was because of Mama. She couldn't let it go. How many times did we try to get her to move? What was it she would always say?"

"I don't have anything to run from."

"Right. And she certainly isn't running now. We've let this place mean too much for too long. Loving Mama wasn't always easy, but selling this place doesn't mean we're letting her go, too. Why hold on to it? We'll split the money. And y'all can do what you like."

Catherine looks at Di and then at Hetch. "But..."

Hetch takes Catherine's hand.

Di says, "It's time, honey. I need a change. There are some things I'd like to do and I got to do them on my own."

Catherine looks confused. "Like what? What do you mean?"

"Well I sure as hell ain't going to shack up with you two

lovebirds."

Catherine holds up her hand stopping the conversation.

"Hang on. Nobody is shacking up. Di, I'm not even sure..."

Hetch leans forward. "You're not getting away this time. I've been waiting my whole life for this."

"But we don't need to rush anything. I don't know that it's best to make any decisions right now. I have things to think about. David is going to get better and he'll need me to be there."

Di leans forward. "Why not? Rush it. Rush everything. All of it. What are you waiting for? Hetch's here, sitting right here where he's always belonged. David might get better, honey, but he might not. He's in a good place. He's where he needs to be. You and I both know that."

Di was accustomed to swallowing the lump that formed in her throat when she was lying to her sister. Di knew David would never get better. She hated to think it. She loved him as if he were her own, but she also saw how deeply troubled he is, always has been.

He was an unpredictable child. He was behind in school not because he couldn't do the work, she knew he could. He was smarter than he let on. He just didn't care. They couldn't ground him, take away TV, his favorite toys, because it made no difference.

The duplex they rented backed up to a wooded area. One afternoon, Di looked through the window and saw David, ten years old, standing in the woods. He was completely still, arms hanging, head slightly down. She could see his eyes, though, looking directly at her. There was no expression on his face. He didn't need one. His eyes said it all. The hairs on her arms stood up. A sharp pain shot through her gut.

David was terrifying.

Di knocked on his door and tried the knob. "David, you

know you're not supposed to lock this door. Open up, please."

"Why should I?"

"Why? Because I asked you to."

"No!"

"Now, David. That's no way to talk. Don't you talk ugly to me, son."

"I'm not your son."

"Open the door."

"You're losing your temper, Aunt Di."

"If you don't open the door, you'll lose your notebooks. All of them. And your pens. Do you want that? Do you want me to take this door off the hinges?"

"Don't lie, Aunt Di. Mama will give them back to me. You know she will because drawing helps me to stay calm. Don't you want me to be calm?"

"Not if she knows how you've been behaving, she won't. I know it was you, David...I know you're the one that nailed the squirrels to the tree. I can't...I don't understand. How could you do that, David?" She banged on the door. "Open this door now!"

He laughed. "You think you're scaring me? You're not. No, I'm the one scaring you."

When he was barely a teenager, eleven maybe twelve, Di forced Catherine to take him to see someone. She'd thought it might break Catherine to do it. Would Catherine blame her? Di risked everything when she put her foot down. She told Catherine it was best for them, for Jo. He was whispering things to Jo, telling her how she could stop the bad thoughts, wouldn't she like to feel something else?

Di threatened to call the police.

"Catherine! Do you know what he's doing? What he's saying to Jo? He's manipulating her. She's got scratches on her arms. She told me how he watched her do it, how he told her not to stop."

"What? Scratches? Like cuts? Why? Why would she do that? He's younger than she is. She shouldn't listen to those things he says. He doesn't mean them. Don't look at me like that, Di! I didn't know. I swear I didn't. But it's not his fault, Di. He can't help it. I'm not blind. I know he's wrong in some way, but you don't just give up on your children. I can't give up on him. He's my son! Don't you see? You can't tell me what to do with my son."

"Yes, and that's why you have to help him. You have to help both of them."

"No one else will understand. They won't see what he's been through, what I've put him through. Doctors will scare him. He's just a child. He can get better here at home. I'll take time off work and give him the attention he needs. If I send him away...what if he gets worse? He's like this because he's angry with me. And why shouldn't he be? I wasn't there. For so long. He needs me now. I can't leave him again."

"You need to look at me right now. Look me in the eyes. Let me tell you how much I love you and him and Jo, and let me tell you that you are dead wrong, sister. If he stays here, he's going to hurt someone. If you don't do this, I will. I'll call the police. I'll take Jo and go back to Wimbee, to Bibba's. And it breaks my heart, Catherine, but I will do whatever needs to be done to protect Jo. And to protect David from himself. I'm done being afraid. And you should be, too."

Catherine made the call and Di believes, saved all their lives.

Di points at Catherine. "And you. You may be fine china, but you're still an antique. Who knows what's next? For goodness sake's. Go find out who you are when you're not blaming yourself for everything. Forgive yourself. We are here to bury our mother. If anything, that should tell you to enjoy the life you've got left."

"It's not that easy, Di. I can't leave it all behind."

"That's the past. And we can't change it. I'm not asking you to forget it either. The reality is your kids are grown. That part of your life is over. It's not that they don't need you, they just don't need you in the same way anymore. Besides, you're not leaving them. Just changing direction."

"I wish it weren't over. I wish I hadn't missed it."

"I know, sugar."

"But what about you? Are we going in different directions?"

"Yes. Because it's time." Catherine reaches for Di's hand. "I might surprise you, Catherine. Maybe I'd like take a cruise, travel, hell, I don't know. Maybe I'd like to see what the moon looks like while sitting on a rocky cliff in Scotland."

"If that's what you want." They sit quietly and then Catherine laughs.

"You'll freeze your ass off."

"The hell I will. Maybe I'll meet a young Scottish lad who'll keep me warm."

Di needs coffee and a smoke. She takes her cup outside and watches Jo move a pile of dirt she's just dug up. She walks out into the yard and puts a hand on Jo's shoulder. They stand together looking down into the hole.

Jo sniffs and wipes her face with the back of her hand.

"Hetch said he'd do it, but I wanted to." The physical labor was good for her.

Di says, "Just told your mama I want to get rid of the house."

"Oh." Jo nudges a rock in the grass with her shoe. Di puts out her cigarette. "How you feel about it?"

"Fine. Couldn't really say it matters much." She looks up.

Di sees the little girl she'd helped in and out of the car, the one she'd taught to cook a pot of rice, and plait her own hair. She can hear her squeal as waves wash over her toes, her laugh while she and Bogue chase away the seagulls, her screams in the middle of the night, and the cold look in her eyes as she lay in the hospital bed after walking into the lake.

"You're not a perfect woman." Di says.

"And you're no Mother Theresa. What's your point?"

Di rolls her eyes. "What I'm saying is, there's a lot that's happened to you."

"There's a lot that's happened to all of us." Jo asks, "Why is it, do you think...why didn't Bibba wait for the cops?"

Di lights another cigarette and takes a long pull. She knows Bibba made a choice. Probably made it long before Ryland showed up and put a knife to her girl's throat. It's the kind of choice someone makes when they can take no more. They're done seeing their people threatened, get kicked around, made to feel ashamed. She was tired of evil winning. Di knows Bibba was going to end it or die trying.

Di an still feel the hard chair she was offered at the police station and the smell of the room. It reeked like a gym, all body-heat and sour socks. Detective Miller sat across from Di, questioning her. He looked like a man who had seen it all. She looked into his dark brown eyes. He knew. He knew things weren't right. He also knew what would happen if Ryland were arrested, taken to prison, given a sentence less than death. He would be back. They always came back. Death was at their doorstep that night or some night in the future.

She watched Miller's face, listened to his voice taking her through the events, going through the motions, doing what he felt like he had to do. Could she relive her mother holding the shotgun? Did her mother know how to live with her choice to end a man's life? Not just a man, but the man that hurt Di's family and murdered her love. How had Di felt sitting in that room with the blank walls, the room where she was asked to let strangers into the darkest moments of that night? She felt relief. It was done. She had faced her fears. He was gone. Nothing could harm her. Her mother had given them that.

It was a gift.

And now? She stretches her arms open and back as wide as they will go. She relaxes with a groan and lets the tension ease away. The morning sun is shining on her face.

Di looks at Jo. "Why does anyone ever do something like that? Revenge? Anger? Sadness? Fear? I think it was because she believed it was the only way. I don't think she could go on living in the same world where he was living. He was breathing the same air. The man that was slowly killing my sister and her children, the man who murdered the man I love could walk down the street and buy a hamburger. He could stop and take a piss in tall grass. He could spit out of a car window. He could go see a movie, buy some popcorn, and sit in the back of the theater with rows of other people. People who wouldn't know the monster that he was. Granted, he'd have to do it while looking over his shoulder, but the point is he could do it.

I think she spent that summer knowing if he showed up, she'd kill him. Her decision was made. I think she knew he wasn't dead when he jumped from the bridge. It terrified her to think he was out there and she knew he'd come. And because she'd already made up her mind, she knew she couldn't let him get away again. He was some inhuman thing, Jo, stalking in the night, growing more powerful with every minute he was left breathing." Di pauses to smoke.

"She couldn't bear it. I don't believe he was the kind of person God intended for this world. I'm not saying what she did is right. Who's to say? But I'm not saying it's wrong either. She did it so one of us wouldn't have to. So you could live."

Jo nods.

"You got yourself a damn fine hole, miss."

"Yep. It's a good hole." They both laugh and head inside.

It's time to say goodbye.

26

Bibba

December 31, 2014

I told myself I'd finish this before the end of the year.

I don't remember at what point my shoe fell off. Memory is a strange thing. Was that real? Did I make that up? Why do I remember the pain of my shoulder hitting the carpet and the burn of the cheap fibers back and forth on my skin, but I can't remember the squeeze of his hand on the back of my neck? I saw the bruises. He must have done that. I can still hear the sound of the chairs knocking into each other, one of them falling over onto the carpet with a thud, but I can't remember how I got home, who drove me.

I imagine that you have moments like this, too. Maybe it's a smell, a sound, or the way someone walks, something you hear on TV, the sound of the lake water lapping at the shore. Could be anything, I guess. I hope you have forgiven me. Know that I love you, Jo. David, your mama, Di. My soul is a light breeze through a field of tall green grass, easy, peaceful, at rest because I know I did what needed to be done.

We don't outlive the bad things. We learn to live with them. Our lives are made up of tiny moments strung together and if we try to cut out a moment here or there, then the string falls loose and dangles in the nothing. We have to keep our strings tied together because it's who we are. We have to focus on the moments that are to come, wanting to get to that next moment because of where our strings lead us. Don't cut your string, Jo. I'm holding the other end, waiting for you.

Jo

They gather in the mid-morning sun. Hetch takes Catherine's hand. His big tanned hand. Jo can't take her eyes from it. Those hands have picked apples in the fall and strawberries in the summer. Hands that stirred pots, raked yards, hung up laundry. They held baby spoons to small hungry mouths and wiped tear tracks off of dirty little faces. They carved animals out of wood, made furniture, held her mother's face. They cut through jungle with a machete, shot men from hundreds of yards in foreign countries, and they carried a woman from a hospital to a car, a woman choking on anguish to the point of self-harm, a woman so deeply committed to her regrets that she could no longer distinguish herself from them.

Earlier that morning Hetch walked over with the shovel, said he'd be glad to dig the hole. Jo declined, but before he gave her the shovel he paused. He wanted to tell her something.

"There's something I've been wanting to say, Jo." He looks down, pushing the shovel into the ground.

"Yeah? What's that?"

"That night. I should have been there. I should have stayed at the house."

"Hetch, no. We all thought he was dead. There's no way you could have known."

"No, but that's just it. I did know. I felt it. You forget, but I knew him and his family, too. I knew he wouldn't go that easy. So, instead of staying to protect you, I went to the bridge. I went to find his body. I needed to see it, to know it was over. But the whole time, he was headed back to ya'll and I couldn't protect you. If I'd been here..."

"If you'd been here, you might be dead and not standing here with that shovel that I now need. And who would have helped Bibba and Di take care of us? Who would have carried Mama in and out of the house? Convinced her to eat, to drink, to come back to us? Nobody else would bring me out in the yard, play catch with me when the feelings were just too big for me to handle. There wasn't anyone else that could have protected me the way you did after everything happened. There's no way I could be the wife to my husband and the mother to my sons that I am without having seen what a good man is. You showed me that."

They stood together with tears in their eyes. Hetch reached in his coat pocket. "I got something for you. Meant to give it to you awhile ago. But I just couldn't seem to part with it." He pulls out a wooden horse.

"You made this."

"Yes. I remembered that you broke the first one. I'd always wanted to make you another one, but things got in the way and before I knew it, ya'll were gone."

"Well. We're here now." She hugged him fiercely.

In the morning light, she could see how much he had aged. She felt a pain in her chest and thought about all the time they'd lost in-between.

And yet. Here he stands, now, with her mother holding the

only hand he has ever wanted to hold.

Jo looks down at the urn. "Wait," she says. The others look up at her. Jo fumbles in her pocket searching for the tube of lipstick she found in Bibba's bathroom. She rolls it up and runs it over her lips, the color a pink flame lighting her face. She passes it to her mother who smiles while she puts it on. Di groans and accepts.

Now they are ready. The urn fits nicely in the bed of dirt. Ashes to ashes. Dust becomes dust. No one knows quite what to say. Hetch covers the urn with earth and then returns to Catherine's side. Jo's mother lets go of his hand and lowers herself to the ground. At first, Jo thinks she will wail or cry out Bibba's name. Jo reaches for her mother, but stops. The little girl in the purple shorts is there, kneeling down beside Jo's mother. The girl places her hand on Mama's back. Then, Jo hears her mother's words: Thank you. Thank you. Thank you.

Later, Mama and Hetch are in the kitchen putting together something resembling a meal because whenever something happens (a birth, a death, a graduation, a divorce) food is a way to care for one another. One can never have too many casseroles or pies, Bibba would say.

Jo is setting the table when she hears a car outside. She walks out on the porch. Di is sleeping in the rocker. Jo slips the lit cigarette from Di's fingers and puts it out.

Jo walks to the edge of the porch. He has never looked better. "What are you doing? Where are the kids?"

Will closes his car door and sets a padded envelope on the hood of his car. He walks a few steps toward her.

"Hi. I dropped them with my dad." He hasn't shaved and his beard is patchy and gray.

After the lake, while she lay considering the shapes of the clouds out her hospital window, he whispered his secrets in her ear. The words flowed in to her brain and rushed through her veins, settling in the curves of her heart. He had become a part of her. Once she was home from the hospital, they walked together, sat together, and she found, in time, she was able to share the details of that night with him, and all the other nights before and since.

She lets the tears fall and walks down the stairs and into his arms.

"Oh, Jo. My Jo. Just let me hold you." He strokes her hair.

She loses all composure and sobs into his chest. His feet are planted and he holds up her weight, letting her fall completely into him. Yes, she is strong enough to do this without him, but why not do it with him? *I will let him carry me again*, she thinks.

"Crying makes you stronger, you know. Scientific fact. Look it up, if you want to." He sways her left and right.

She pulls away from him slightly so she can see his face. She's a mess. Her hair is oily, her face is swollen and red, and her nose is running. "Sorry", she says wiping her nose on her sleeve.

"For what?"

"Oh, everything, I guess."

"Okay. I accept. But don't apologize for this," he motions to the house, "All that you went through isn't your fault. What you show me is who you are. I know the person I married, Jo. I married all of you, not just your easy parts, but your uneasy parts, too. Just like you did for me. We're doing all of this together. There isn't anything about you I don't want to see or experience. I'm not afraid. Are you?"

"Only of losing you. You've been distant lately. I've been wound up over all these changes. There's been a divide. And maybe it's something we can overlook in the day-to-day, but when the shit really hits the fan, I can't manage without you."

"You can. If anyone can, you can."

"But I don't want to."

"Won't happen."

"Promise?"

"I already did. But, yes. Over and over again." He kisses her forehead. "And I'm sorry, too. I just know how capable you are. See, I still remember that fourth grade girl I used to watch while hiding behind the big oak tree on the playground. She was quiet, but had this presence, like she could take on anything and win."

"You never were very good at hiding. I saw you every time."

"I should have been here from the start, Jo."

"You're here now."

"I never wanted you to feel alone."

"I know."

They sit down on the stairs together. Will takes her hand. "Brian says 'Hi.'"

Jo punches his shoulder and smirks.

"You know what it is, don't you? He's just trying to find his own way. And because you're the most important thing to him in the whole world, the one that he knows will love him no matter what happens, he can test the limits. You're his life-line. He can pull away knowing that he can always come back, that you'll always pull him in if he needs you."

"Right. And because I suffocate him. I know I do. It's just hard to give the kids the space they need. It scares me."

"That's why God made dads. It's parenting with less suffocation." He grins. "It scares me, too."

Jo looks surprised.

"What? You know me. It might seem like I know what I'm doing on the outside, but in here I'm a ridiculous mess when it comes to you and the kids. If there's a problem, I want to fix it fast and inevitably, I say the wrong thing or I push too hard to get through the emotional part so that we can get to the fixing part. I'm a classic case."

"So you are."

They sit on the steps for a few minutes, leaning on each other until Di yells at them from the porch to quit smooching and come eat.

"How did you know to show up?" she asks.

"Di called me."

"Of course she did. Are you hungry?"

"I could eat."

Jo stands and holds out her hand to pull him up. She looks up at Di and smiles. Di waves and goes in the house.

"You know, I've been watching Mama and Di, really looking at them. And I've always thought they were beautiful, similar looking, but not the same. Definitely sisters. And I could never find myself in them. But something is different now. They're more beautiful than ever. Softer, maybe.

Could be all the crying is blurring my vision. But, I'm beginning to notice small things like the shape of our fingernails, or the way Mama can't walk in a straight line. I can't either. I've caught my reflection here and there, when I've got something on my mind, and I've seen the same expression on Di's face many times. Maybe I'm just paying more attention.

I think I've focused for so long on the ugly and miserable ways in which we're all connected. I don't want it to be like that. I want the happy stuff, too, the sweet and good stuff. They're getting old, Will."

Will pulls Jo in for a hug. "They've always been that beautiful, Jo, and so have you. If I'm being honest, I think it's you that's softened. And out of all three of you, you're the one. You've done a lot of work to get here, to the point where you can see yourself included as one of the grown women in that house. They're just waiting for you to join them."

Jo takes a deep breath and nods.

"Oh, hey before I forget..." Will goes down the stairs toward his car and grabs the brown padded envelope. "I hope you don't mind that I opened it. It's from Bibba's lawyer's office. I got worried. I wanted to look at it before you did to, you know..."

"Protect me?"

"Yeah."

Jo lifts the flap and pulls out a small book. It has a plain black cover. It's not a book, but a journal. Bibba's journal. She flips a few pages and stops because there is a photograph tucked in the front.

"Is that Bibba?" Will points at a girl in the photograph. She is leaning against a fence, young and fresh and gorgeous.

"Yeah, it's gotta be. Some kind of picnic at the church, looks like."

She flips a few more pages stopping to read what she knows is a hymn. She can hear Bibba's humming while she reads:

O' God this night, thy face is near
Through shades of darkness, your presence here
With weary arms, I cast my sins upon your sea
And the tempest passes o'er me
I close my eyes and find restful sleep.

Will takes her hand and she feels her palm press against his. She feels the space between them disappear and knows the pieces of their lives fit together to make something new, something different, something better.

ACKNOWLEDGMENTS

First of all, thank YOU for reading this book. It's an indescribable feeling (even for a writer) to know that his or her work is in the hands of a *real* reader. Thank you for giving me the opportunity to tell you a story. I'd like to thank my friends, non-writers and writers alike, who have listened, given feedback, encouraged, and acted like they cared every time I talked about this book and the process of writing it. Thank you to the #WritingCommunity on Twitter and Instagram, a group full of talented writers and creators. Don't give up! Also, thanks to the #5amwritersclub for the donuts. Thank you to my parents for what feels like a thousand years worth of love packed into thirty-something. To my mother specifically, for reading draft after draft and editing each one with the same amount of excitement and enthusiasm as the first. Your guidance and support are irreplaceable. Finally, thank you to my husband, Justin, my-only-love, my-forever-love for understanding why I need to write and reminding me to keep my chin up because I'm worth it. And my two sons, Jack and Ben for making me a mom, which gave me the perspective I needed to see these characters for who they are.

It's been a long decade of writing.

ABOUT THE AUTHOR

Alissa lives in Hillsborough, North Carolina with her husband, two sons, mother, and three dogs. MAD MOON is her debut novel.

For more information on Alissa, please visit www.alissacmiles.com.

You can also find her on Goodreads.com. Come by and say, "Hey!"

Twitter: @alissacmiles
Instagram: @alissacoopermiles

CPSIA information can be obtained
at www.ICGtesting.com
Printed in the USA
LVHW042331290820
664253LV00005B/394

9 780578 702544